THE GUIN SAGA

Book Three: The Battle of Nospherus

KAORU KURIMOTO

TRANSLATED BY ALEXANDER O. SMITH

WITH ELYE J. ALEXANDER

VERTICAL.

Published by Vertical, Inc., New York.

Originally published in Japanese as *Nosuferasu no Tatakai* by Hayakawa Shobo, Tokyo, 1979.

ISBN 978-1-934287-06-4

Manufactured in the United States of America

First Paperback Edition

Vertical, Inc.
1185 Avenue of the Americas 32nd floor
New York, NY 10036
www.vertical-inc.com

Much time will pass before the pattern is revealed—and yet it exists entire from the first fold of the skein and reed. Sages are those who see patterns in the threads.

—Akmet, the Book of Prophecy

CONTENTS

Chapter One

WHITE DEATH

I

Nospherus—

The very name was an omen of evil, an invocation of phantasmal terror. It was the domain of the demon Doal, and few who crossed into his forsaken wastes alone ever returned to the Middle Country. It was called a no-man's-land, for although many mortals lived there, none of them could truly be called "men." The closest, perhaps, were the Sem, small creatures that looked much like monkeys and sported tails as furry as the rest of their bodies. The only other humanoids were a fabled race of giants who stood more than a few times taller than the Sem—the barbarous Lagon, who were equally hairy, but who were even less intelligent (it was said) than their simian cousins.

In its climate, too, the hot outland of Nospherus was far different from the homelands of humankind. There were hardly any seasons, the thirsting landscape never knowing the spring grace of green leaves or the brightness of fresh blossoms.

It was a desert waste, its bleak badlands perennially cloaked in stone gray and dust-brown.

To the east of Nospherus rose the lumpy ridges of the Kanan Mountains, while to the north lay the eternally snow-capped peaks of the Ashgarn range, beyond which were the icy Northlands. Along the southwest flowed the Kes, the black flow that separated Nospherus from the outlying settlements of the lands of men.

Thus hemmed in by natural borders, Nospherus had come to host an unusual and unique kind of life. Wildling human-oids lived side-by-side with all manner of monstrosities: sand leeches, sandworms, bigeaters, giant scorpions, wispy angel hair, foul yidoh...

These foul yidoh! thought Istavan the Crimson Mercenary. *Whatever madness it was that drove Archduke Vlad to covet this accursed land, I'll bet he'd change his mind if he saw this!* He grimaced and looked out on the bizarre sight before him. It was worse than anything even the boldest kitara players sang about in their fanciful tales of heroic deeds.

Istavan, his friend Guin the leopard-headed warrior, and the forty or so warriors of the Raku tribe whom they led had followed the young Captain Astrias's routed troop of Mongauli knights to the last plain where the wildlands dipped down towards the River Kes. There they had seen the main host from

Alvon Keep marshalling for action, a massive army augmented by reinforcements from Torus and led by the Lady of Mongaul, Amnelis herself. It had become apparent then that the duchy had finally launched its long-planned invasion of Nospherus.

With no less than the survival of the Sem tribes at stake, Guin, Istavan, and the Sem scouts, intent on warning their comrades, had made haste toward the village of the Raku. But it seemed that the aged weaver Jarn, heavenly guider of fate, had other plans for them. Perhaps he felt that they had not been tested enough.

Though pressed for time, the party had had to run north to throw their Mongauli pursuers off the trail. When they finally turned east and toward the village, it was into a far greater danger than that from which they fled.

For whether the Raku guides had taken the wrong path, or the land itself had shifted to baffle their progress, what they now found before them was not the village of the Raku, where the twins of Parros, Rinda and Remus, their faithful companion Suni, and the high chieftain Loto awaited them. Instead, they had marched into the midst of a colony of primitive jelly-like creatures—yidoh—that undulated now as one eerie mass. By the time the quick-moving warriors realized their plight, they had gone far into the valley. The dread creatures swarmed and oozed perilously close to them.

"What is this? How—" rasped Istavan, his voice hoarse and grating from thirst.

"Not so loud," Guin hissed. The yellow eyes peering from his leopard face narrowed and shone with startling ferocity. "They know something is here, but they have not yet sensed what we are, or they would have moved in for the kill." Guin's voice was low and calm. None understood better than he that his life, and those of Istavan and the forty brave Sem youths, depended on him keeping his cool and making the best move.

For Guin was their undisputed leader, though he had never been appointed as such. There was no need—from the beginning it had seemed natural for them all to entrust their lives to him. Although Guin did not know this yet, a rare ability to lead was as much a part of him as the strange leopard mask that covered his head. He was one of those very few to whom others turn for leadership, guidance, and protection as if by primal instinct, and the wont of such a one is to bear the burden without expecting so much as a promise of loyalty in return. So spontaneous was his compassion and sense of responsibility. And without a doubt, the lives of Istavan and the Raku rested in his hands now.

Guin glanced back swiftly. The Raku youths remained calm, or at least, appeared so. The sight of the leopard warrior riding tall at their helm gave them heart, and Siba, the foremost among them, was skilled at keeping order. The Sem gazed warily upon the roiling reaches of the valley of death, and stood silent in their ranks, holding their breath, waiting for Guin's orders. They knew from experience that while the yidoh were fearsome carnivores, they were not as aggressive as the bigeaters or the sandworms. For the moment, waiting quietly was the wisest course of action.

"Now," whispered Guin in a low voice, "we go back. But we will not turn yet. We must keep our faces forward, and retreat one step at a time. Walk slowly until we reach…that bend in the path with the reddish rocks. There, we turn and run out with all our speed. Once outside the valley, we will wait for any who have fallen behind. Good? Move as one, and move quietly!"

"Yes, Riyaad," came the Sem warriors' hushed reply.

While he spoke, Guin never shifted his eyes from the yidoh filling the valley. The primitive forms quivered and surged, like too much jelly in too small a pot. The entire valley floor was covered.

An ancient, primal form of life, the yidoh were possessed of neither eyes nor mouths; nor were their bulbous shapes equipped with appendages of any sort. Their lack of jaws and sensory organs made them no less dangerous, however. Like giant white amoebas grown to an illogical extreme, they sensed— and fed—with their entire bodies. Now, numberless, they flowed together, soundless and slick, so that the valley was filled with a translucent white pool that rippled and murmured. It was impossible to say where one yidoh began and another ended, for wherever two of the creatures touched, one would engulf the other, even as, on its opposite side, another yidoh was splitting into two new masses. This they continued endlessly.

"And I thought I'd seen it all," muttered Istavan, gently backing his horse to follow the Raku warriors on their slow retreat.

Guin replied without a trace of humor in his voice. "Remember, mercenary—no spitting. They may not have eyes to see us, but they know prey has entered their valley. If one of them tastes a glob of warm spittle, they'll all be on us in a flash."

"Doal's arse," Istavan swore under his breath and kept moving backward. He remembered all too well how it had felt when one of the amoebas had latched onto his leg back in the desert—an experience he had absolutely no desire to repeat. The turn in the path where the reddish rock jutted out seemed farther away than before, though they had not taken a step. He imagined the mass of yidoh launching themselves into the air as each reacted to the prospect of something more succulent to digest than other amoebas, and fear churned in his stomach.

Yet the stealthy band of warriors did reach the bend in the trail after what seemed an eternity of slow, backwards shuffling.

There they turned as one and ran like runners at a fair, Istavan and Guin bringing up the rear on their horses.

Siba and the other Sem were the first to reach the exit of the narrow gorge that led into the valley. There they waited in tight formation. Their round eyes shone uneasily, and it seemed that they were huddling together as much for reassurance as for defense.

"Riyaad!" Siba came running over to Guin's side.

"All your men are unharmed?"

"Unharmed, Riyaad."

"This valley of the yidoh—did you not know of it?"

"No, I had heard, but—" Siba made a sour face. He had led the party astray, and the guilt made his ears burn and his throat dry. "They were not here before. That is certain. The yidoh move," he explained. "They moved, and came to this valley."

Guin nodded thoughtfully. "Hmm. Surely you are right. The creatures must move far during the night in search of food, leaving nothing whole in their path. Their coming here is not your fault. We were unlucky."

"Yes, Riyaad." Siba's hairy face showed a mixture of shame at his own failure as a guide and relief that the party had escaped unharmed.

"Hey, Guin, what's the monkey saying?" asked the irritated Istavan.

Ignoring him, the leopard-man said in the Sem language, "We must go around. I hate to delay our arrival any further, but anything is better than sitting here."

Siba exchanged looks with the Raku standing next to him, then turned back to Guin, shaking his head. "But we cannot go around, Riyaad," he said.

"What?"

"There is this valley, then another valley, and then there is the village of the Raku. Riyaad said we must hurry, so I showed you the one path, the secret path that goes straight to our home. There is no other way through the mountains from this side."

Guin thought in silence.

"Guin? What do we do?" Istavan demanded in a vexed tone. "What's he saying?"

When Guin quickly translated Siba's message, Istavan guffawed and said, "You're kidding! By the gruesome ghouls of the Roodwood, I've had enough of those yidoh to last me a lifetime. Let's backtrack some more. There'll be a way around to the east if we get out of these hills."

"Mmm," said Guin, thinking. "That we cannot do."

"Huh?" Istavan raised an eyebrow. "Why not?"

"If I were a Gohran captain, the entrance to these hills is just where I would leave a full troop to catch anyone coming back out."

"Ah...that's right. We were being followed, weren't we?" Istavan muttered. The mercenary swore a silent oath and glared at the hills that barred their path.

"That, and we're running out of time. Look—the sun sets."

Guin hunched his shoulders. Istavan looked up to see the Marches sun slipping behind the top of the mountains. In the rush of their flight, he had forgotten that night was coming. The wildlands night, deep and unforgiving, boded great danger and darker mystery.

The huddled Sem warriors peered uneasily up at the setting sun and occasionally cast questioning looks at Guin. Their eyes were filled with trust and loyalty toward the leopard-headed warrior, but there was also fear.

"I couldn't have planned a better trap," Istavan observed, grinning as if it were someone else's pinch. The seasoned mercenary was no mere rat. "We go forward into the valley of the yidoh, or we go back and the Gohran host cuts us to ribbons. There's no third way on account of these bleeding hills. What's more, it's growing dark, and if we don't get to the Raku village, our friendly wildlings could be taken by surprise and put to the sword, the lot of 'em. So, my leopard-noggined generalissimo," said Istavan with a flourish of his hand, "whatever do we do now?"

Guin growled deep in his throat.

The mercenary added in a grumble, "Tell you one thing—I'm not becoming any yidoh's dinner."

Guin raised a hand, palm upward, as if to say he held no secret means of getting them out of their predicament.

Istavan shook his head and looked up into the deepening violet of the Marches sky. "What's with all the angel hair, anyway?"

Since they had stepped on the road that led down into the valley, the wispy white angel hair had been falling thicker than usual, and now it formed a veritable fog on all sides. Though they knew it to be harmless, the sight of the white tufts descending on them did little to soothe their frayed nerves.

"By the white beard of—" began Istavan on another tirade of colorful oaths, when a thought struck him. His black eyes sparkled. He leaned over and slapped a hand down on Guin's shoulder. "I've got it! Why didn't I think of it before? It's so simple. We use fire—fire! By the sulfurous spittle of Migel, that's it! Didn't you say when you saved me from one of those things before that fire was the only way to deal with the yidoh? We'll just burn a path through the slimy sons of—"

"And send up a beacon of smoke the Gohrans are sure to see?" interrupted Guin, who had already considered that option some time before.

Istavan scowled and fixed his leopard-headed companion with a glare. The former pirate's obsidian eyes flared in the gloaming. "Fine, then what *do* we do? We could just walk back and forth in this valley until one of our enemies finds us. And we all know the yidoh move at night."

"That, they do."

"Yeah, so what—"

Guin raised a hand to silence the mercenary. "Siba!"

"Yes, Riyaad?" All the Sem grew suddenly tense, ready for action. They could tell that Guin had made a decision.

Guin gestured to Istavan, and the mercenary reluctantly leaned closer. The leopard warrior looked over his companions once, then said, in the tongue of the Middle Country:

"The fate of all the Raku hangs on our every move. We have no choice. We must cut through the valley of the yidoh."

2

Istavan, and even Siba and the Raku warriors, stood staring at Guin, speechless.

The mercenary finally wrung the words out of his dry throat. "Wh-What did you say?" He coughed. "We cut through? Yidoh?!"

"Yes," Guin said sternly. He repeated himself in the language of the Sem, and there was a commotion among the ape-men.

"You jest," protested the mercenary, "and poorly at that!"

"I make no jest."

"Then you're mad, by the twin faces of Janos that rule the holy light and the darkness," Istavan declared with a cold finality.

"Crimson Mercenary," Guin said, his voice rising a little, "we're running out of time." He then turned to Siba and spoke with him a while in the language of the Sem.

"What was that about?"

"They make their home here in Nospherus, so I asked them if they know of any scents or herbs the yidoh dislike. Perhaps we could rub something on our skin to repel them."

"Har! If it were that easy, then—" Istavan proceeded to mock, but Guin raised his hand to quiet him.

With a serious look, Siba turned to speak to his fellows. They conferred briefly, but when he turned back to Guin, his eyes were clouded with disappointment.

"Perhaps our elders know some secret, Riyaad, but we are young..."

"I see." Guin did not sound particularly surprised.

"Wait!" said one of the younger Raku, shuffling out from behind Siba.

"You are?"

"Salai, Riyaad. I, too, have not heard of such an herb, but I did hear something from my father's father once, long ago. He said that the Sem of Nospherus once used to tame the yidoh, the riyolaat, and the mouth-of-the-desert to do our will. We used magic, and the creatures listened, and obeyed."

Guin growled and his eyes took on a thoughtful look. It was an interesting story, but not one that seemed of much use to them at present. In response to Istavan's pestering, Guin translated the words of the young Sem.

"Bwah hah! Magic?" the mercenary snorted. "If I had

magic, the last thing I'd be doing is hanging out here with night coming on, teaching the yidoh tricks! If we can use magic, let's just fly over that cursed valley and be done with it!" He chortled bitterly, but suddenly his eyebrows furrowed. "What is it, Guin?"

"If that's what we must do, then do it we shall," the leopard-headed warrior stated calmly.

Istavan looked at him with eyes round as saucers. "Do...what?"

"What you just said we ought to do: fly over the valley and be on our way."

The mercenary shook his head in disgust.

"Istavan Spellsword, I am not saying we should sprout wings and fly across as though we were balto birds," the leopard-man explained. "Nor could we leap over the valley, it's at least a tad in length. But no such feats are demanded of us. All we need do is keep above the yidoh."

Guin repeated himself in the Sem tongue, and then gave a number of instructions to the Raku, leaving Istavan wondering what plan there could be. The Sem bowed their heads attentively and listened. Then, as one, they looked up and leapt into action.

"Wait, wait, what's going on here? Would it kill you to let me in on things for once?" Istavan complained. A clump of angel hair slapped across his mouth just then, and he had to brush the stuff away with his hand.

Guin peered at the silken white wisps with interest. "Might it be that angel hair always appear where there are yidoh? Much like the tiny fish that always gather around the shark in the sea."

"A fine time for natural history, my leopard-headed friend!"

"At ease, mercenary. We have not yet seen the pattern that Jarn's spinning wheel weaves for us tonight."

Istavan stared at Guin, who stood with arms crossed, his mask as always expressionless. The mercenary declared, in the petulant tone of an upset child, "How you can act as though you're lying by your own hearth, when we're in Nospherus, I have no idea—unless you really do hail from this no-man's-land!"

Just as Guin was about to respond, Siba and several of the other Sem came running up to him with clinking loads of gleaming things between them.

"You found some?"

"Yes, Riyaad!" The Raku dropped their precious cargo before him.

Leaning in curiously, Istavan knit his brow and said, "Crystal? What for?"

It was a pile of strange, elongated rocks, crystalline in structure, which the Sem could find protruding from the bare slopes because the valley was far enough in the north. The slabs of crystal had been broken off with great care.

Guin had asked the Sem to bring the clear but hard stone, in as long and slender a form as could be found. The Sem had split into several groups, each group bringing back a load of slender fragments, many longer than the Sem themselves were tall.

Testing the strength of the crystal-rocks in his hands, Guin noted, "This would be easier if there were some tall, sturdy trees about, but Nospherus isn't kind to anything that grows much higher than our Raku friends here."

"What exactly do you have in mind?" Istavan's black eyes were wide as a child's as he stared, nearly in pain with curiosity, at the rocks in Guin's hands.

Guin's answer was simple: "Stilts."

"Stilts?"

"Yes, though I do not pretend that crossing the valley on these will be easy. Even with the crystal veins giving them strength, these rocks are thin and brittle, and cannot be cut too long. Also, I fear that, thin as they are, they may yet be too heavy for the Sem to use with any ease. They may also be too fragile to support you or me."

"I don't get it," Istavan confessed.

Taking great care not to shatter them any further, Guin selected two sections of crystal-rock, one very long and one very short, and, taking a length of the sturdy vine-rope that the Raku used to bind their bows and arrows, proceeded to tie them together so that the shorter one stuck out perpendicular from the larger one about one-third of the length from its top. His large hands moved with surprising dexterity as he made one and then another of the contraptions.

Guin tested his improvised stilts to make sure they were sturdily fixed, then he waved to the tallest of the Raku, the one called Salai who had spoken earlier. Guin instructed him in the language of the Sem: "Salai, place your foot here at the cross-piece and try to stand. I'll hold you."

"Yes, Riyaad." Salai sprang up with agility and stood on the poles, making him taller even than Guin who stood supporting the slender sticks of stone.

"What do you think, Salai? Can you walk with these?"

"I will try, Riyaad," said the young Raku warrior. As soon as Guin released his hands, Salai began to walk, holding the tops of the two stilts one in each hand. He lifted each leg slowly and swung it carefully forward, taking one small step at a time.

Immediately the other Raku gathered around, finally understanding Guin's plan. It seemed that Salai was naturally very agile, even for a Sem, for after falling once or twice, he appeared to get the hang of it.

"Can you walk through the valley like that?"

"I can try, Riyaad. Yes, I think so. But these pole-legs are very heavy." Salai jumped down from his stilts and caught his breath. "Siba and I will be able to use these, but I fear that Mano and Cai and others do not have the strength…"

"I will not be able to use them either, Salai. Nor Istavan here. If we tried, those brittle poles would surely break," Guin replied. "But all of us need not go. That would take too much time, and besides, we do not have enough of these crystal-rocks to make pole-legs for all of us. One or two of the bravest Raku will go." This last part Guin repeated in human speech for Istavan's benefit.

"So they'll run ahead to the village, while we just wait here?" Istavan interceded.

Guin shook his head. "No, I have another plan for the rest of us."

"By your leopard-headed god-sire Cirenos, you've gone and figured out a way for us heavier folk to cross, too, haven't you?"

"I…think so. It involves some danger, though."

"Well, I'm beginning to think that you'd have something up your sleeve even were you to face Doal himself." Istavan said this coolly, but a sparkle of admiration danced in his black eyes.

"Riyaad?" Salai had approached slowly, and now stood by Guin, waiting for instructions.

"It will not be easy," Guin told him, looking down at the small, hirsute face. It shone with determination. "Have you the courage, Salai, to cross the valley of yidoh?"

"Yes…Riyaad, yes!"

"Should you lose your balance, let a tired leg slip—or should this valley be much longer than we guess it to be—you will fall head first into the yidoh."

"I-I understand." Salai shivered, but it was with anticipation, not fear.

"The fate of the Raku—no, of all the Sem—rests on your making it across that valley alive," Guin added softly.

Then he gave a signal, and two of the Raku brought a long rope that they had made by linking bow-strings, carrying cords, and belts. Guin tied one end of the rope around Salai's waist and held the rest looped in a long coil in his hand.

"You will carry your end thus to the other side. Let us also tie your feet loosely to the pole-legs so you do not slip… Ah, and one more thing…" Here, Guin pulled out a torch. "Bring this. I know not how long it will keep you safe, but should you slip and fall, you can use this to burn away the yidoh."

"It is fine, Riyaad." Salai flashed Guin a toothy grin. "If I fall, Siba will make it across in my place."

Guin silently placed his hand on the little Raku warrior's shoulder.

Salai was ready to go. It was something of a suicide mission.

To make himself lighter he had left his bow, arrows, and stone axe behind, along with most of his clothing. The rope that the Sem had prepared was tied about his waist, both his feet rested securely on the footrests of the stilts that Guin held steady, and the torch was affixed to the top of one of the crystal-rock poles. Salai looked back at Guin and his companions, gave another bold grin, and signaled that he was ready to depart.

"Let us go. I will carry Salai up to the edge so he will not tire before he begins."

Guin made sure the other Sem were prepared for their tasks. Then he picked up Salai, pole-legs and all. Watching his steps carefully, Guin headed down into the valley of the yidoh, carrying Salai cradled in his right arm. Behind him, Siba, Istavan, and about half of the Raku followed at a distance, stopping to watch where the last bend in the path concealed them from the widening valley—the exact place where they had begun their dash to escape not long before.

Guin moved slowly to the edge of the expanse of swarming yidoh, set Salai down gently, and looked out over the squirming mass.

They seemed much the same as they had been before, yet

they were constantly changing. The fearsome, shapeless creatures continued their eternal undulation, the vast, nightmarish
pool that they formed heaving with discontent, moving and
rippling like the surface of a windy lake. Again and again, each
individual yidoh stretched questingly outwards, only to retract
and meld in with the others once more. A careful observer
might have noted that these sickeningly pallid jellies were not
consistent throughout. Spherical shapes were visible within
each, and convulsing crescents, thicker and more opaque than
the rest of the mass—the yidoh's barely developed organs. It was
impossible to tell from the endless swirling and twisting
whether the foul things had noticed the intruders. Impossible,
too, it was not to sense hunger from them, an insatiable
hunger.

Salai stood looking over the eerie living sea that he would
soon cross, his eyes betraying no sign of fear. He took a few
steps on the stilts to test out his fittings one last time.

"Make it to the other side," Guin commanded simply.

Salai nodded. "Yes, Riyaad."

Then, moving on the crystal stilts with skill, as if they were a
natural extension of his own legs, he ventured out into the valley of the yidoh.

At some point, Siba had come up behind Guin, who stood
staring grimly out at the yidoh. "You should not stand so close,

Riyaad. Dangerous." He tugged urgently on Guin's arm with a small furry hand.

"Hmm? Yes," Guin murmured, moving back a short ways, but not as far as the safety of the canyon-corner, where a dozen round furry faces watched from behind the wall of reddish stone.

The valley was now quite dark, and at the bottom of that darkness the innumerable pale bulbous shapes continued to writhe and grope. It appeared that the yidoh could be faintly luminescent—and yet, evidently, they were capable too of blending in with their surroundings. The yidoh that had attacked Istavan during their first night in the wildlands had been as dark as the nighttime rocks.

"Dangerous, Riyaad," Siba warned again, tugging on Guin's arm.

Guin did not move. His leopard face was an expressionless mask as he stood watching Salai's progress. The brave Raku was like a tiny boat adrift on a pale luminescent sea. The lone torch struggled against the pressing darkness, blinking like the eastern star that guides men's travels. The elite Sem warrior moved slowly and deliberately, choosing each step with care as he passed through the very middle of the yidoh colony.

Salai's feet were less than two Sem's height above the top-most of the yidoh. Every time one of his stilts came down, the yidoh around its base would squirm in search for the intruder in their midst. But they found no living thing, and because the creatures were not particularly viscous, Salai had little difficulty freeing his other pole in turn and lowering it anew into the writhing mass, each step bringing him that much closer to the unseen far side of the valley. As he made his way, the cord tied around his waist stretched out farther between him and Guin. With great care Guin paid out more rope from the coil around his arm, neither letting it draw too tight nor sag down and touch the yidoh. At times this was the only proof of Salai's progress, which was painstakingly slow. It seemed like he would never be free of the deadly sea.

Suddenly, a gasp went up from the watchers. Salai wobbled—he had lost his balance.

"Ah!" even Istavan let out a cry, fearing the worst. But the agile wildling somehow managed to get the stilts back under him and regained his delicate poise.

"Riyaad," Siba stretched up and whispered to Guin. "Riyaad, I will practice so that I may go, too."

"Do so," said Guin, never taking his eyes off Salai. The leopard-headed warrior seemed calm, but the sharp-eyed would have caught the trembling of tensed muscles under his bronze, sunburnt skin. His clenched fists, too, contradicted his aura of composure. "Yes, prepare yourself. I only hope you will not have to go," said Guin, so softly that none—not even Siba, who was already heading back to practice—heard him. *If we fail once, then fail again, we are finished. Even if we could gather more crystals, we are fast running out of rope, and only a few torches remain. Even if we unstrung all the bows we'd only get one more chance at best...* Not voicing this, instead he stood watching Salai's perilous trek with all the confidence of one who has a solution for any problem, a plan for overcoming any difficulty.

"He's not through them yet?" swore Istavan behind him. "In the name of Doal, how far does this blasted swarm stretch?"

Guin looked down at the rope in his hands, the lifeline connecting them to Salai, and saw that it was running out. If the yidoh colony extended for any more than a tad, the rope would not span it, and Guin's plan would fail.

He shook his leopard head, trying to clear it of dark thoughts. It was when he trained his eyes on Salai again that he heard the Raku's wildly joyous shout. "The other side! I see it!"

"Guin!"

"Riyaad!"

A cheer rose up from Istavan and the Raku warriors. A growl of relief came from Guin's throat, and he went into a half-crouch, squinting to see across the sea of yidoh. Some time before, Salai and the torch he held had disappeared over a low rise midway along the valley floor.

"You're almost there, Salai!" Guin called out into the darkness. They had nearly run out of rope, but apparently there was just enough.

"Keep alert!" Those were the exact words Guin was about to add when a scream echoed across the valley, a spine-chilling scream.

It was Salai, and the horrid cry could only mean one thing.

"Salai!" Guin shouted. But the rope had gone slack in his hands.

Salai had fallen.

— 3 —

"Salai!" Guin shouted, but the darkness swallowed his cry.

"Salai!"

"Riyaad!"

Guin hauled on the rope with a mad strength. At first it resisted, like a fishing line pulled taut by a heavy catch, then suddenly it grew light and came as quickly as he could pull. Drawing in its end, he scrutinized it closely, and then tossed it down behind him in disgust—the rope had caught on some rock along the way and had frayed until it snapped.

"Riyaad!"

Guin turned around to see the small, worried faces of the Raku. He shook his head.

"What happened, Guin? Did he make it?" demanded Istavan as he hurried near.

"He did not," Guin said solemnly, in words the Sem could not understand.

The Crimson Mercenary tried in vain to peer through the murk that had settled over the valley. "The poor monkey…"

"It will not take long. Thankfully, the yidoh are very efficient at what they do," Guin muttered. Then, looking up with a jerk, he motioned violently for Istavan and the Raku to retreat. "Stay back—come no closer! They have noticed us!"

Istavan did not have to be told twice. Swiftly he ran back to the safety of the bend in the canyon. Behind him, the white mass that filled the valley was rising in a storm of activity. It seemed as though the entire colony of yidoh had sensed the feast that their brothers on the far edge had received, and now the rest of them were pulsing and stretching to see if there were tasty morsels within reach. Some of them had started in the direction of Guin and the others. It was a sickening sight.

"Keep your distance," growled Guin, herding the Raku farther back along the canyon like a sheepdog directing a reluctant flock.

"Riyaad!" It was Siba, making his way through the retreating Raku. In his hands he held a length of rope and a torch. "I will go next."

"Salai's sacrifice has told us one thing," Guin said grimly. "We now know how far it is to the other side of the valley. You have a little less than a tad to go—about fifty motad past the curve, no more. Pace yourself accordingly." He did not bother to add empty words of encouragement to that.

"I will succeed," Siba declared fiercely. The death of his comrade had not quenched the brave wildling's spirit. Then, perhaps to cheer the rest of the Raku, he observed, "I am stronger than Salai was."

"Have you mastered the pole-legs?"

"Easier than taunting a sand leech, Riyaad."

Siba would have set out immediately, but Guin made him wait until he had double-checked the fastenings on his crystal stilts and adjusted the hang of the rope at his waist. Taking the loose end of the rope, he tied on to it what remained of the coil that had linked him to Salai.

"Alphetto, your protection," intoned Siba. Then he was off into the valley.

The remaining Raku huddled close behind Guin as they watched their companion leave. They were nervous. They understood the importance of this second attempt, and Siba was one of their most respected warriors. The death of Salai was fresh on all their minds. It seemed that the yidoh, too, remembered, for while they had left Salai's stilts largely unmolested, they now wrapped their pseudopods around Siba's at his every step, searching for anything edible. Siba was forced to lift up his crystal pole-legs quicker than he would have liked. Many times he nearly stumbled, sending a gasp up from the watching

Raku, only catching his balance at the last moment.

But Siba was agile, and he was progressing away from them, slowly but surely, to the other side of the valley. Guin looked upwards and away from Siba once, as though to supplicate the heavens for help. He saw faint white wisps of angel hair falling from a starless, charcoal sky.

"Hey, Guin," Istavan came up to him and whispered, "what you got planned if this one doesn't make it?"

"I'll know then."

"Come on, I know you better than that. I know you've got something up your sleeve."

"Maybe," Guin allowed, "but Siba will not fail."

"How do you know? Have you now the spirit-sight like little Rinda?"

Guin did not respond. His eyes were fixed on the torch atop Siba's right-hand stilt. "If he can just make it past there..." Guin muttered, half to himself, "and if we can follow...then we—and the Sem—will have an edge. It is already dark, yet with our Raku guides, we can move with relative ease, while the Mongauli's forays will be greatly hindered. They will have to close ranks and set watch against the dangers of the night, and wait for the morning to come before they march on. Our tracks will be even harder to follow after a night of the hard winds blowing down from the Ashgarns...and they do not know the exact location of the Raku village. Even if they do succeed in following us, with any luck the yidoh will still be here. What better guard to set at our gates than...*this?*"

"Let's hope it's not so good a guard that it keeps us from getting through, eh? Speaking of which, I bloody well hope we get across soon. These jellies may be hungry, but so am I!"

Guin did not bother answering. Swiveling his leopard head, he scanned the valley. Siba was already lost to their sight. Thanks to the extra rope that Guin had added, the coil in his hand was not running as thin this time. Still, a great deal of rope was now stretched out into the pale luminescent darkness above the yidoh.

"If Siba fails, we will have to return to where we entered these hills." Guin said this in a near whisper so the Raku would not hear him. Though they could not speak the human tongue, they would be alert to his tone, and he could not let them sense his uncertainty.

"But what about the Mongauli?"

"It will take time and it will not be easy, but if we can slip back under the cover of night, there's hope that we'll be able to take the Mongauli by surprise, even if they've set an ambush. We can cut through, and then go around the mountains. It's a long way to the village, but it may be the only way. At any rate, none of the other Raku have the strength to cross this valley—

Siba is our last chance."

"Guin! Have you got a yidoh for a brain? Have you forgotten how many thousands of troops are out there?"

Guin suddenly sprang to his feet.

"What?" Istavan said, taking back a step.

Without answering him, the leopard warrior ran straight up to the very edge of the yidoh. His voice high and strained, he called out: "Siba!"

There was a terrible moment's silence. Then a cheerful cry answered him, "Riyaad!"

"You've done it, Siba! Are you all right?"

"I am fine, Riyaad! I have crossed the valley!"

"Siba! Siba! You did it!" roared Guin, laughing as he turned to tell the other Raku.

But there was little time to celebrate. Moving quickly, Guin gave directions for the next stage of his plan. He knew that Siba was already following his instructions on the other side: fastening the rope to the highest point which he could find and checking to make sure that it would not come loose no matter how hard it was pulled.

On his side of the valley, Guin climbed to an outcropping of rock he had noticed earlier that jutted out high above the path. There, taking care not to snap the rope with his great strength, he fixed it tightly around an upthrust horn of stone.

The rope now hung in the air, suspended at both ends and crossing the valley diagonally, forming a modest bridge to the other side. Guin faced the far end of the valley and called to Siba. Siba responded with a cry, and Guin pulled on the rope a few times to test its strength.

He nodded, and muttered, "It will do." Then he returned to where the remainder of the Raku waited to hear what plan their resourceful Riyaad had devised to save them. He looked around at the faces of the Sem, and said to them, "Thanks to Siba, who risked his life for us all, a piece of rope spans the valley right now." Then he asked, in a tone that was almost harsh, "Do you have the courage to cross the rope-bridge?"

"Yes, Riyaad!" the Raku called out as one.

"Wait now," Guin raised his hand. "This is no river crossing or mountain climbing. The valley is wide, and you must cross the whole distance with your hands and your feet on that rope. Fail, and you will meet the same fate as Salai."

The Raku were silent. Yet, one by one, they raised their hands to the sky to say they were not afraid of the fate the gods had chosen for them. They were ready.

Guin looked them over and nodded. "Then the lightest of you, with confidence in the strength of your arms, should go first." Giving this order, he stepped back.

The Raku looked at one another, sizing up their companions, until one of the smallest of their number clambered up the rocks and took the rope in his hands. He moved out onto the rope until he was hanging by his hands and feet like a jungle sloth. Then, with remarkable speed, he began to wiggle along the rope, bending and stretching like a tree-worm.

Istavan shivered and cursed, "I'm not so sure about these plans of yours, leopard-head. The yidoh are going to have a feast tonight. Delivered to them, no less! How many of us do you think can make it across on that poor excuse for a bridge?"

"You are forgetting," said Guin, checking the knots in the rope for any loosening or fraying against the rock, "that our friends are Sem. Is it not you, Crimson Mercenary, who calls them 'monkeys'? Their arms are as strong as their legs, and they have less than half our weight to support. Crossing on this rope is a challenge for them, but not a ridiculous one."

"For them, sure, but in the name of their smelly monkey-god, what about us?" Though he took a step toward Guin as he said this, his tone was not really accusatory. "Well," he continued, not waiting for an answer, "I'm sure you've got some plan even if we can't make it across on that rope, you being you and all. By the hundred squinting eyeballs of Jarn, you are a tough one to beat, Guin. Here I was thinking we were bound to go on a fruitless walk through the wilds of Nospherus, and you came up with that crazy stilts idea. And it even worked!"

Guin was about to reply, but instead reached out a hand to stop the next Raku from climbing onto the rope. "Let the heavier ones go now—first, the next heaviest after Siba."

Already, six of the smaller Sem had made it to the other side of the valley. Crossing on a rope suited them far better than walking on stilts, and they were travelling more swiftly than Istavan had thought possible. Yet already, one of the Sem had slipped and fallen. A surging crest of the pale jelly that was the yidoh had enveloped him as his companions watched; he had become a featureless lump of flesh in mere moments and was nowhere to be seen in the slime.

"We have to send some of the heavier ones across now, while the rope is still strong," Guin explained to Istavan. "Should it begin to fray, the lighter the load, the better."

"Why not strengthen the bridge with what's left of the bowstrings?" the mercenary offered.

"I've considered it," Guin replied, tilting his head thoughtfully, "but we'd not have enough for—ah, it is ready!"

With an air of importance, several Raku who had been busily making something came up to the outcropping.

"Good, cross now, and hurry," he told them. Most of the forty Sem had gone already. "How many have fallen? Six? That's on the lower end of what was to be expected." He shook his head and watched the last Sem head out over the sea of yidoh one by one.

"How holds the rope?" Guin called out.

"It is fraying halfway across, where it rubs on a rock, Riyaad! Elsewhere it is strong."

"The fraying, is it bad?"

"It will hold!"

"Okay," said Istavan, irritated by the chittering, none of which was comprehensible to him. "So the monkeys are doing fine, great. What about us? You're not going to ask me to wiggle along on this thing, are you?"

"I think we can do better than that." Guin pointed at the last two Raku, who had just climbed onto the rope. They had a cord attached to their waists. As they began to make their way across, the cord grew taut and began to lift up something that had lain on the ground below the outcropping.

It was a net, quickly and simply made.

"What in the world…" let out Istavan.

"You will ride on that. We are too heavy to cross the valley as the Sem did, but with the help of this net—which the Raku will pull from the other end—we should be able to make it. Of course, we'll use our own hands and legs too, on the rope."

Istavan peered at the wildlings' handiwork. The Raku had done a fine make-shift job. The net hung evenly like a merchant's cargo bag, and at the top formed a sliding loop on the rope. Through it ran the cords that were tied to the waists of the last two Raku, who were briskly making their way across the valley. From the other side they would be able to pull the net towards them.

The tall mercenary of Valachia, deserter from the Marches patrol, stood for a while without saying anything. Glaring skeptically at the contraption, he reached out a hand and gave it a firm tug. "You're telling me to hang above the yidoh on this thing? By the sulfurous fiery breath of Doal! Back when I was a pirate on the Lentsea, I used nets like these to transport goods, even a few servant girls, between ships. No time to put up a proper gangplank when there's fighting going on, you see." He pursed his lips, and then elaborated, "Sugar bags, casks of wine, gold dust in leather pouches, clothes. The fellows who've boarded the ship stuff it all into a basket and pull on the rope to say it's ready, their mates haul it over, and that's all there is to it! By the Godwyrm Dridon, caretaker of the sea and the pirates who ride her, I never thought I'd see the self-same piece of wisdom up here in the hills of Nospherus—and with me as the loot! And this time, instead of the gentle blue and wine-mild sea-mother below me, I get an ocean of squirming slime that'll eat me for dinner if I fall in." He scowled and was silent for a moment. Then he waved his hand and concluded sulkily, "Fine, fine, I'll get in the damned thing. It better work!"

Guin let out a howl of laughter, despite the fix they were in.

Istavan was the "Spellsword," the "Crimson Mercenary," barely turned twenty but wise beyond his years in the ways of the world and the trials of battle. At heart, nonetheless, he was just a mischievous youth whose spirit still frolicked on the sun-drenched shores of his natal Valachia. Now and then he made Guin laugh hard, but it was not a mean-spirited or condescending laugh. They were bursts of pure mirth.

Istavan shot a hostile glance at the laughing leopard-headed warrior. "Still," he said, sounding more optimistic, "I know for a fact that there's not a chance in the world I'll meet my end at the hands—or whatever they are—of these yidoh. When I came into this world, a gem in my hand, the fortune-teller said I'd one day be king. So sure of it she was that she named me after a great king of old, and I'm no king yet. Until I do get my crown, it means, I need not fear death! No stinking valley of jellyfish can take me to the underworld yet! Yup, yessir, I'll get on the net, I'll be the booty if you insist!" And with this contorted piece of logic, he clambered up the rock nimbly toward the net.

"Wait," said Guin, stopping him.

"What now?"

"Take off that armor. The Raku said that the rope was fraying. You'll want to be as light as possible."

The mercenary shot Guin a look like a maiden who had

been asked to do something most improper. But without a word, he began undoing the straps of the black Gohran armor. One by one, he threw the chestplate, the greaves, and the gauntlets down onto the hard ground, until his slender form was clothed only in his leather boots, his short trousers, and the padded undershirt that had fit close under the armor.

"I can keep my sword, can't I? Without it I'd feel more naked than if I'd taken off all my clothes," muttered Istavan. Glowering, he crawled into the makeshift basket, where he looked like some giant fish caught in a fisherman's net. "I don't know if it's Mos, Cirenos, or Doal himself, but pray to your god for me, leopard-head." With this, he grabbed onto the cord and gave it a good tug.

This was the signal. In a moment, the rope, which had sagged under Istavan's weight, pulled taut. With the combined strength of the Sem tugging on the cord and Istavan pulling hand over hand on the rope as he sat in the basket, the hastily constructed transport began to move out across the valley with surprising speed.

"Whoa! Watch it! Yipes!" yelled the mercenary with every sway and lurch. His eyes bulged wide as he looked at the swirling, slimy creatures that writhed not a man's height below him. Istavan was considerably lighter than Guin, but still, he was at least twice as heavy as the largest of the Sem, and the makeshift bridge had already held many Raku. *And dropped a few*, the mercenary thought glumly. If it sagged any more than it had already, his feet would hit the yidoh, which were stretching yearningly toward him!

"Uggh," groaned Istavan. "By Irana's seven tails, I hope this is a first and last time. Please, you yidoh just rub me the wrong way!" He reflexively drew up his legs until he had nearly curled himself into a ball.

The yidoh had begun to move again, a disturbing ebb and flow. Salai, who had sacrificed himself, and the six Raku who had fallen from the rope had been consumed entirely by now, but that had done little to sate the eternal hunger of the yidoh. If anything, the meal of Sem had made the gruesome creatures hungrier, and they lurched and lashed out with bulbous pseudopods. They were more active than Istavan had seen them all night, surging and heaving in deadly waves.

As a single mass they pulsed back and forth across the valley, reaching up the rocky sidewalls with furious violence, driven by their blind hunger. The entire mass was sensing for shifts in temperature and sent out pseudopods of yidoh to test whether the things they crashed against were inedible rocks and trees or warm, living food.

Istavan's sun-tanned face twisted in a grimace of disgust. The net in which he sat, which had moved so quickly at first, now seemed to advance with appalling slowness, and the mercenary began to despair of ever reaching the end of the fearful journey. Tired of looking down at the sea of yidoh, he peered back up at the rope against the dark sky—and his wearied face went pale.

"Gah! The rope, it's fraying!" Istavan gave a terrified howl. "H-Help! Help me gods, I'm going to fall!" The mercenary's obsidian eyes opened wide as he stared at his only lifeline, the single rope that held him above the valley.

He had only made it two-thirds of the way, still a considerable distance from the safety of the far side where the Raku stood waiting for him. The basket shuddered, and he looked up again. Before his eyes, the makeshift rope was fraying, the wound cords splaying faster and faster.

And then the rope broke.

— 4 —

"Ahhhh!"

From opposite sides of the valley, Guin and the Raku heard Istavan's terrified cry, yet they could do nothing to help him.

"Gods! Mos! Jarn! Anybody!"

The rope had been strong, but after bearing the weight of forty Sem, its worn fibers were too weak to support Istavan. He was almost within sight of the valley's far side when it unraveled and snapped.

Tangled in the net, the mercenary dropped straight down toward the horrible sea of yidoh in the valley below. Rather than fight for his life to the very last moment, he screamed, screwed his eyes shut, and covered his face with both hands, as though by doing so he could avoid confronting death.

It was a short fall, though to him it felt like eternity. Legs wrapped around the rope that was no longer there, he tumbled down through the murk, until he finally landed.

He screamed and curled himself into a ball, though he knew this would not help him once he was seized by the yidoh, whose touch would quickly dissolve any living tissue. Yet the pale, luminescent, jelly-like creatures did not grasp him; his helpless body was not engulfed; the terrifying death did not come.

Istavan slowly opened his eyes and peered out between his fingers into the horrid night. Then, all of a sudden, he pulled his hands away from his face and sat up.

"Unbelievable," he croaked, his mind reeling with surprise. "By the shining hair of Irana who watches over me! This is…"

Unharmed save for a few bruises he had gotten from the fall, and without a single yidoh attempting to consume him, Istavan struggled out of the net and stood up on the soft ground of the valley.

He opened his black eyes wide, straining to see through the darkness around him. The nearest yidoh had already slithered far from where he stood. "Well I'll be… They're moving! They moved!" shouted the incredulous mercenary. Then he started laughing hysterically. "By the blue pot of Aeris from which the moonlight spills! By the fever brought by Torto, the god of lovers, what luck, what *luck*! No—not that I expected any different! Why, I'm Istavan Spellsword, I am! Luckiest man in the world! No stray arrow of misfortune will ever hit me!"

And lucky he was, for the yidoh had begun to flow out of the narrow valley the moment he had begun his crossing. Had the fell hive set out even a *twist* later, the Crimson Mercenary would surely have fallen squarely in their midst.

Like a night tide, they were now surging down the narrow canyon along which Guin's band of warriors had come, oozing back towards the low wildlands of Nospherus. When Salai and the other Sem had fallen, some primal instinct had been triggered in the shapeless monsters that prompted their primitive instinct to seek more food. As a single mass, tads long, it seemed, they were gliding away to the southwest. Like an amorphous larva newly hatched from its egg, the hungry swarm had blindly made its way away from Istavan and the Sem.

The mercenary looked around again and noticed that he was still too close to the retreating yidoh to warrant much celebration. He swiftly scooped up his fallen sword and made haste to get out of range of any strays. His eyes fell on something left lying on the valley floor in the yidoh's wake—a small pile of bones. Doubtless they belonged to Salai, who had died that the rest of them might cross the valley.

Istavan shivered. The remains were hardly recognizable as such. It looked much as Istavan assumed the victim of a giant jungle snake might look if you cut open the snake's belly a few days after it had made its catch. The yidoh suffocated their victims with their huge, formless mass, then crushed and digested them until only piteous lumps of twisted skeletons remained. Istavan looked at the whitened bones and a tingle ran up his spine. *It could have been me…*

"Well, no sense thinking about that," the mercenary muttered. "I didn't end up as yidoh fodder, and by the white gossamer of Aeris I'll keep on living, thank you very much." He shook the visions of grisly death out of his head like a dog coming out of the water, then leapt over the few rocks and boulders that lay scattered on the ground between him and where the Raku were waiting in a worried huddle.

"Lo, my furry friends! I made it! Don't look as though you've seen a ghost. It's me!" the mercenary announced, unconcerned that they could not understand his words nor he their reply.

Indeed the Raku, their eyes wide and round, paid him little attention.

"Riyaad!"

"Riyaad! Enee, reek, rahnee!"

"Riyaad…"

The Sem fretted in their high voices, peering back through the darkness of the valley.

Istavan wrinkled his brow and looked back the way he had just come. "Guin?"

A sudden realization came to him. *That's right—Guin's still on the other side! And damn if those yidoh weren't heading his way!* He looked around frantically for some way to bring his friend to safety, but the erstwhile bridge lay in a ragged tangle on the ground, leaving Guin stranded on the wrong side of the valley.

Istavan peered through the gloom toward the mouth of the narrow canyon, wracking his brains. For a moment, a strangely pained look stole across his haggard face, but he shook it off and spat on the ground. "Ah, no need to get all excited. He's fine. My monkey friends, Guin is fine! Why, if all the yidoh in the world attacked him, he'd still pull through! Anyway," Istavan paused to wet his lips and continued, "shouldn't we be getting along? We don't have time to just stand around here, do we? We have to get to your little village. We'll just start walking slowly and Guin will catch up."

But the Raku didn't understand what he was saying, and besides, no one was paying him any attention at all. In fact, all of the Sem warriors were still pointing out into the darkness toward the other side of the valley, and talking animatedly in the high-pitched voices of theirs.

It seemed to Istavan that they were debating whether or not they should go back into the valley in order to save their Riyaad, back into the very place they had just crossed with so much difficulty and death. Already the leopard-headed warrior was more of a god to them than a man, and it occurred to Istavan that they might just be willing to give up their own lives in an attempt to save his. Siba in particular sounded quite vehement. He waved the single remaining torch in his hand and chittered passionately, perhaps rallying the entire band to charge into the valley and burn a path through the yidoh to Guin.

"Hey, hey, bad idea!" yelled Istavan. "You can't seriously be thinking of burning the yidoh out of there. Why do you think we went through that whole mummers' act to get over them in the first place? If we lit a fire big enough to drive them off, the blaze would have the whole Mongauli host upon us in a flash. Look, I'm telling you, Guin will manage. He has to!"

The Raku seemed unconvinced, if indeed they understood him at all. Forty pairs of angry eyes, in fact, glared now at the Valachian mercenary.

"H-Hey, now, no need to look at me like that," he stuttered, blanching and taking a step backwards, when suddenly one of the Raku screamed.

"Alphetto!"

The tiny warriors' eyes bulged with fear, and they hurriedly scattered in all directions but one, back into the valley.

Istavan turned and saw what had caused the Raku to run, and he was stuck to the spot, petrified with fear, his tongue stuck to the roof of his mouth. He could not tear his eyes off the nightmarish thing striding slowly toward him.

A shape like that of a great sea monster out of some horrible myth was rising from the yidoh, parting them in two. It was like a mass of yidoh in human form, with its arms outstretched. And it was coming directly toward Istavan.

"G...Guin?!" Istavan yelled and ran towards the human form, then stopped, unsure of what to do. If he moved any closer to the yidoh, they'd be on him for sure.

It was indeed Guin who had come inexorably up out of the sea of yidoh. Every inch of his mighty form—even his leopard-masked head—was covered by yidoh, so that it was impossible to see any of his features, but Istavan did not doubt it was Guin. Lunging suddenly, the yidoh-Guin reached out and snatched the torch from Siba, who alone out of the Raku had stood by Istavan instead of running off. The little Sem yelped and jumped back, while Guin turned the torch and thrust it at his own head!

His body, still covered with yidoh, now erupted into a ball of flame.

"Yaaah! Guin!" Istavan yelled.

The figure in flames twisted and scraped at its sides as though in great pain, then dropped to the ground and began rolling about furiously. The flames went out as fast as they had spread.

"What in Doal's name..." The mercenary stood, mouth agape, unable to speak a word more. The Raku, too, watched dumbstruck, forgetting to do anything but stare.

Guin—or the figure they believed was Guin—lay there on its side, and for a while did not move. The blackened remains of yidoh were plastered all over the giant frame, smoldering in the cool night air.

Istavan swallowed and found his voice at last. "Guin... Guin! You...didn't burn yourself to death, did you?" He smiled uneasily, and his voice trembled.

Then the crumpled form twitched, and the head lifted ever so slightly off the ground.

"No," came the familiar growl, only thicker than usual, "I am not dead."

"Guin!"

Only then did the fear that had held Istavan and the Raku frozen in place finally release its grip. All at once they gathered around him to see how badly he had been burned.

"I am fine, give me space to stand," the leopard warrior grumbled, his voice becoming clearer by the moment. Suddenly, his hand went to his face and pulled off the blackened shell that covered it.

Istavan and all the Raku gasped as one. Guin's round leopard head was unharmed, his golden whiskered visage barely singed by the heat of the fire. Guin chuckled. "I'm lucky the flames died when they did. I thought I was going to suffocate. Luckier still that Siba thought to stand there with his torch like that. It was the only thing I could see through the yidoh covering my eyeslits." The warrior's yellow eyes blinked and shone, and he cast down the husk in his hands.

It was a piece of the black Gohran armor that Istavan had taken off before crossing the valley. Guin had worn the chestplate over his mask, and with that as his shield, charged straight through the yidoh!

Istavan whistled and shook his head, amazed. "By the many miracles of Janos, are you a man of flesh and blood? To charge headlong through the yidoh like that, then set fire to your own head!"

"I had planned to do that from the start—and I dare say, my journey went smoother than yours, Crimson Mercenary!" Guin gave one of his characteristic howls of laughter as he worked busily to remove the rest of the armor and blackened yidoh remains from his body. Istavan stared at him, and snorted.

As soon as Istavan had started out across the valley in the netting basket, Guin had hastened to gather up what slabs of crystal remained. These he had tied to his torso with leftover bowstrings and cords from the horses' bridles. This makeshift armor, together with Istavan's greaves and gauntlets, had protected his bare flesh from the yidoh's powerful digestive juices, and with the chestplate fixed over his head so that he could see through its fastening-slots, he had made his way across the valley.

"That was a little too close," Guin admitted after he had finished discarding the last piece of armor. "I need some wine."

He lifted the wineskin that was put into his outstretched hand and drank deeply. "Those yidoh were stronger than I imagined. I had to tense every muscle just to keep from being crushed, and I knew that if they knocked my feet out from under me I was done for. I took the last torch and burned a path before my feet for most of the way, but I dropped it... I took a deep breath and charged for the last thirty motad or so. Five paces more of those things, and I would have run out of breath, or lost my footing."

"You're a bigger fool than I thought, Guin! I don't care how strong you are or how long you can hold your breath. Your standing here alive is nothing but the most incredible, unbelievable piece of bleeding luck I've ever seen!"

Guin laughed. "I knew from the beginning that our rope would not support my weight. So you see, I had enough time to consider how to protect myself for a race through the valley."

"By Mos' grassy whiskers!" whispered Istavan. His black, sparkling eyes were filled with a look of wonderment that had never truly graced them before, and although he would never have admitted it, his eyes also betrayed a profound relief at seeing Guin standing before him again, safe.

"Though I can't say I made it unscathed," the leopard-headed warrior noted, "this is no worse than a few Marches bug bites." Guin sat and examined his body carefully. Here and there, blisters were rising on his hands, feet, and chest; and on his sides where the yidoh had pressed with bone-crushing force, the crystals had shattered and their points had driven into his flesh. Guin let Siba and the other Raku place compresses over his wounds, and he stretched and rubbed his stiff neck and shoulders.

"Those horses deserved better," he said, looking over the dark void of the valley from which the shining luminescent sea of yidoh had disappeared without a trace. "I set them free, but I fear the yidoh have caught and eaten them. If I hadn't been so preoccupied with getting myself ready for the crossing, perhaps they wouldn't have had to die."

"Aw, Guin, what difference does that make? Haven't you and I gotten through?" remarked Istavan, a little vexed with the leopard-man. A short distance away, the Sem had built a small fire, cutting a little globe of warmth out of the cold Nospherus night. Istavan gazed at it plunged in thought; and in the firelight, his black eyes shone almost chillingly with their customary shrewd gleam, as if to balance out the warmth that had recently filled them. How could he have guessed, when he first heard Guin's raspy voice through the prison wall back in Stafolos Keep, that only days later he would be here, in the hills of Nospherus, watching thirty monkey-men huddled around a campfire, and nearby, several more tending to the wounds of a warrior with the head of a giant leopard? The mercenary surveyed the scene and sighed impatiently.

"Better the horses than us," he reprised. "We almost died back there."

"But we did not. We lived—most of us, at least," Guin observed. As much as he would have liked to honor the dead, they had no time to build a cairn for the brave Salai and the other fallen Raku. Guin lightly brushed off the simian hands that tended him, and stood and said to the Sem warriors, "Very well, let us get going. We did not have much time to begin with, and the troubles we had in crossing this valley used up much of what was left. We should have sent a few ahead of us to the village as soon as they reached this side."

"I have done this, Riyaad," Siba informed him proudly. "A party from the village should be on its way to meet us."

"Ah, splendid! Good thinking, Siba," rumbled Guin. "Now we too must set out. It cannot be much farther."

Beaming, the little warrior nodded. "Yes, Riyaad, we need

only cross one more valley and the Raku village will be before us."

The Sem quickly made ready to resume their journey. Some scurried to gather up what remained of their supplies, others kicked dirt on the fire until it was smothered.

Istavan walked up to Guin. "Let's hope those yidoh see fit to head all the way down the hill and eat up the Mongauli army for us, eh?" He said this in a roguish tone, but his eyes were cold and deadly serious.

The band of warriors ran through the darkness.

Faced with the peril of the yidoh, they had almost forgotten the greater danger that threatened all of their people. Now, once more, the Mongauli host loomed in their minds and spurred their feet onwards, making them ignore their fatigue.

Siba pushed himself to run faster to catch up with Guin, who was in the lead, loping like a giant tawny tiger leading a pack of agile hunting dogs.

"Riyaad," the Raku said, his voice filled with concern. "The dark one—is he truly a hero?"

"You mean Istavan?"

"The dark one is not like Riyaad. He screams like a woman, and he talks too much, I think. He wanted to leave you behind, on the other side of the yidoh, even though we could never have crossed the valley without you! The dark one is your friend, so we welcome him…but is he truly a hero?"

Guin laughed out loud, drawing glances from the Sem in tow. "He is fine the way he is, Siba, though you may not understand why," the leopard-man responded between chuckles. "Not all heroes are the same. Some are like Istavan. Yes, he is an uncommon hero!"

Siba seemed unconvinced.

"Guin, cut the monkey talk and look over there, that's got to be the greeting party!" yelled Istavan, blissfully unaware that he had been a subject of debate. Catching up with Guin, he pointed down the sloping path.

There, near the bottom of the valley, they could see the winking lights of watch fires wavering in the night winds. Nearer at hand was a group of small figures waiting alertly with torches held high. Guin's band had arrived at the village of the Raku.

Chapter Two

THE GATHERING OF THE TRIBES

—— I ——

"Riyaad!" Siba's voice trembled with unconcealed joy.
"Our village!"

Siba looked up at Guin, more than twice his height. Beside
the leopard-man stood the mercenary Istavan, also much taller
than the Raku warrior, but wiry next to Guin's impressive
form. The three had paused at the entrance to the valley, looking down on the village of the Raku, which lay nestled in a
cradle of low hills.

The night was deep. In the other valley, little had stirred
but the yidoh and the ever falling wisps of the angel hair, but
here above the Raku village they could see small lights moving
in many places, flickering like sea-fires on the night ocean.
The news of the band's arrival having reached the village a while
ago, the sleepy community had been roused to prepare a grand
greeting.

"Huh, their village looks a lot larger than I expected,"

Istavan said. The idea of becoming a guest of the monkey-like Raku had rendered him uncharacteristically taciturn, but now, with a whistle, he had broken that silence.

A cluster of flames broke off from the pool of light that marked the central village. It began moving towards them. Several Raku were coming up to meet them, holding torches aloft in their hands as they scurried up the slope of the valley path.

"Riyaad! Riyaad!"

"Siba!"

Their cries sounded clear in the night air. Above the voices of the Sem could also be heard two voices that piped in the human tongue.

"Guin!"

"Oh, Guin!"

Two figures emerged running out of the greeting party and did not stop until their arms were wrapped around the leopard-man, hugging him with all their might. It was Remus and Rinda, the royal twins of Parros.

"Guin, Guin! I'm so glad you made it! We were so worried!" Rinda, forgetting her regal manners, and heedless of all else around her, clung sobbing to the leopard-headed warrior, her beautiful silver hair rubbing against his abdomen. Remus, too, hung affectionately onto Guin's waist. The two were like lost baby birds returned at long last to the shelter of their mother's wings.

"There was no need to worry, children," growled Guin.

Istavan cast a baleful glance at the happily reunited trio. He spat disdainfully, "Ah, so the princess of Parros is just a teary-eyed kid after all." Rinda lifted her head from Guin's torso, and as if noticing the mercenary for the first time, looked over at him.

Istavan, expecting the usual curt retort, was surprised when she said nothing. Rinda merely exchanged glances with her twin brother, and the two laughed as if they were privy to some private joke they did not care to share with the Valachian.

"Ech, what's this?" Istavan sneered. "Fine then, go ahead and laugh. Easy enough for you to do! You've been sitting pretty here, royal guests at a monkey banquet table, while my plebian ass was on the brink of death itself!"

"I'm sorry," Rinda replied, still giggling. "Where are my manners? The whole village has been waiting for you. They've prepared quite a feast."

"Yes, a real feast!" chimed Remus. The twins exchanged looks again, and burst into peals of laughter.

"I see you've caught monkey fever and gone mad," declared Istavan, but the news of a feast cheered him up considerably. Young though he was, the long string of adventures and brushes with death had taken their toll; he was very tired, and more than anything, ravenously hungry. As they continued down the slope toward the village, surrounded by torch-bearing Raku who lit the path for them, giving them a heroes' welcome, the Crimson Mercenary softened his scowl. Gazing down at his worn undershirt and leggings, he began to mumble to himself, as was his wont: "Hardly dressed for a feast, am I? True, it's just a monkey village, but would they have stolen armor, from the Marches patrol or something? Just a breast-plate would do. By Sarina Goddess of Beauty's silver-rimmed mirror, I'm a sight to behold."

Meanwhile, Rinda and Remus, for whom Guin the leopard-man was already much more than a traveling companion, nearly clung to him as they made their way. Since the three had met in the Roodwood by chance—or perhaps by some design of fate, one could not know—they had faced the Black Count Vanon, witnessed the fall of Stafolos Keep, braved the treacherous waters of the River Kes, and made their way through the dangers of Nospherus. Guin's past was cloaked in mystery, he himself not knowing who or what he was, but to the twins he was a guardian spirit, and they trusted him with their lives. The twins had lost their parents and their country, but as long as Guin was there to protect them, even the great unknown of the Marches held no true terrors for the homeless orphans.

The Raku had spared no luxury in welcoming the twins. By nature a warm people, they were all the more hospitable when they heard that Rinda had saved the chieftain's granddaughter, Suni. For the first time in the interminable days since the fall of Parros, the twins were able to wash their hands and feet and eat their fill of good food. Yet until Guin was with them, they could not relax.

"Everything will be fine now that you're here!" Rinda oozed. Laughing, she skipped along and led Guin toward the Raku village by his giant hand. But a cloud fell over her smoky violet eyes when she saw the fresh scars on Guin's arms and chest. She stopped, and in a worried tone asked if he was hurt.

"It is nothing," Guin assured her, and spoke no further. His thoughts were on the Mongauli army, and his leopard eyes burned with an impatience that he could not hide.

"Riyaad!"

A new group of Sem, also bearing torches, approached them. At their head trotted little Suni, and her grandfather, Loto, the high chieftain of the Raku. Loto's graying fur glistened like silver needles in the torchlight.

In the cultured words of the Middle Country, Loto said slowly and formally, "Brave warriors, our village and all its people welcome you. We are forever grateful."

Guin raised a hand to interrupt him. "We must save for-

71

malities for later, high chieftain. I need you to summon the leaders of all the Sem tribes, now. Send out word, and may the messengers be quick. The lives of your people, and of all the Sem, depend on it."

Loto's eyes went wide. "Of what do you speak?" he demanded, falling back into his native tongue. A tremor ran through the crowd of torches around him. "You mean not only the Raku, but the salt-valley Karoi, the black-haired Guro, the spotted Rasa, and the yidoh-kin Tubai?"

"That is so," Guin replied, continuing down the gentle slope toward the village, the twins of Parros clinging to his sides.

Flustered, Loto sped up his pace so he would not be left behind. As he trotted along he looked at the leopard-headed warrior carefully to see whether this was some sort of jest, or whether Guin was truly serious.

"Riyaad! Tell me. What is happening?"

"The Mongauli are marching on Nospherus," came the leopard-man's stern response. "An invasion army has already crossed the Kes, ten-and-five thousand in number. They camp on this side of the river and wait for dawn. General Amnelis, the Lady of Mongaul herself, leads them. Judging by that, and by the store of gear they carry and the array of their camp, I believe that they plan to demolish all the Sem of Nospherus: to hit you so hard no Sem will ever cross the river into Mongauli lands again.

Once they have done this, they will likely stay and claim the lands of Nospherus for their own, thereby pushing the border of Mongaul many tads to the northeast."

"Ten-and-five thousand!" Loto rasped under his breath.

A great commotion went up among the Raku who had pressed around them to hear the exchange.

The high chieftain silenced them with a gesture. "Then, the Sem are finished. Riyaad, the Sem will be destroyed." His voice was strangely calm.

It was Guin who raised his voice in anger: "Do not let them! You Sem may be subhuman, or primitive, but to assault a peaceful tribe like yours to satisfy a lust for expansion—no, Mongaul does not have the right. We must fight, Loto! And to fight, we need all the Sem tribes!"

"Yes, Riyaad," Loto concurred softly. And for a while, they walked on in silence.

They were now at the entrance to the village. The Sem community, lit here and there by torches, was comprised of simple dwellings, little more than mounds of shaped earth, like bowls turned upside down and lined in orderly rows that stretched to the edges of the valley bottom. In most of the doorways, Guin could see Raku tribespeople huddled in clusters, peering out at the unusual visitors as they passed.

They proceeded along a road that had been hard packed by

the passage of many feet, through what appeared to be the center of the village. The glittering eyes of the Sem followed them all the way. One word could be heard clearly in the high-pitched chittering, the Sem word for "leopard." Waves of whispers followed them down the street.

"Riyaad...Riyaad...Alphetto-son!"

"I don't believe this!" said Istavan, who could not remain silent for any stretch of time. Looking around uneasily, he drew close to Guin and whispered in the leopard-man's tufted ear: "Hey, Guin..."

"What?"

"Welcome to monkey town! Phew, what a sight! Don't tell me you seriously believe these guys stand a mouse's chance against fifteen thousand Mongauli soldiers! I don't think you do, Guin. Just be nice and tell me you don't!"

Guin was silent. Ahead of them, Loto had stopped. He was signaling now for everyone to gather around him. They were standing before one of the inverted bowl-like dwellings, which, though only dimly visible in the darkness, was clearly considerably larger than any of the others surrounding it.

"Brave heroes, guests of the Raku, I welcome you. Allow us to show you our hospitality," Loto pronounced. Then he grasped Guin's arm with a small furry hand and spoke more quietly. "Riyaad, this way, please."

Guin nodded.

"I'm starving all right," Istavan informed no one in particular, "but first I want some water to wash my hands and feet—and some wine to wash my mouth." Ducking his head, he went into the dark hut first after the Sem.

The twins, who seemed familiar with the place, followed. Rinda turned around at the threshold and looked at Guin as though she wanted to tell him something. But she thought better of it and just flashed a lovely little smile. With Suni at her heels, she stepped in after her brother.

Soon enough, the guests' voices rose up merrily. Istavan's rang above all others, and his voice was full of glee. Their high spirits spilled to the street.

Guin, who had gone in last, glanced over at the mercenary and chuckled. "He is truly a remarkable man, that Crimson Mercenary. How he resisted becoming the guest of the Sem, how he complained! Yet now that he is here, he behaves as though he has lived in this village all his life. It is a rare man who can be at ease in that manner. I would think he is fated for a kind of greatness." He said this more to himself than for Loto, who sat at his side and looked up at him questioningly. The leopard-man's eyes had taken on a stern, resolute look by the time he returned Loto's gaze. The mysterious warrior lightly raised his hand and pointed in the general direction of the arid plains beyond the hills—and the threat that moved there.

"Loto, every minute is precious." Guin's voice was crisp, leaving no room for debate. "Send your messengers, and in the meantime, assemble all the Raku chieftains."

The aged high chieftain nodded, then gestured to an attendant who scurried outside the hut to send the runners out through the torchlit streets. Then he and Guin stood up and left the hut and the sounds of merriment behind them.

The moon rose over the forsaken no-man's-land of Nospherus. Aeris' pale gemstone shone with a clear, lonely smile, beaming down on the dark, oppressive rocks and empty sands of the landscape below. Her light fell, too, on the Raku village, clustered deep in the folds of its hidden valley, but the soft radiance brought no peace. Tonight, there was tension in the air; it was a sleepless night for the Raku.

At the very center of the village, surrounded by rows of mound-huts, was a large, circular clearing. This was the village heart, a space for gatherings and ceremonies. The domed dwellings immediately adjacent to the clearing were considerably larger than those around them.

Guin was ushered into the house on the east side of the clearing. Once inside, he saw that the floor—which was no more than the dirt of the valley itself—had been hollowed out, and a charcoal pit had been dug at its center. A fire burned in the pit, casting wavering light around the room and across the faces of the lesser chieftains and warriors who sat along the edges of the hut. Loto had summoned them to hear the leopard-man's report.

Guin's huge frame seemed out of place in the Raku dwelling, and he had to walk nearly bent in two, but once he reached the fire pit and sat, legs crossed, he seemed much at home.

"The other guests will be well cared for by our women," said Loto, sitting across from Guin. There was not a single ornamentation within the room or upon its walls—it was a simple hollow carved out of the earth and supported with timbers—but several wolf skins had been laid out by the fire's edge. The Raku women brought jugs of wine and delicacies in an endless stream.

Guin and the Raku high chieftain sat talking, heedless of the feast being laid out before them.

"Riyaad," said Loto, with much seriousness. "In the history of the Sem, bands of the painted demons of Mongaul have crossed the river to threaten us many times. Every time, we have fled deep into the wilds of Nospherus. Of course, some of our kind have also crossed the river many times to attack them. These are the Karoi and the Guro. But we, the Raku, we have never faced the painted demons. Why do they not leave the Raku unharmed? Why can it not be that the humans live on their land, and we Sem on ours?"

"Mongaul wants Nospherus for its own," Guin replied.

"Why would they want this place? They themselves call it a no-man's-land more foul than their Marches... They could not settle these rocks, could they? They could not live here?"

"Indeed, they could not," Guin agreed, nodding. The firelight shone on his giant leopard head, casting a round, wavering shadow on the wall of the hut behind him. "I have considered this question for a long time, too. Why would Mongaul turn its eyes towards the wastes of Nospherus? One answer is that, if they were to march on the Middle Country, they would need to ensure that their back was well protected. Should one of the lands in the Middle Country form an alliance with the Sem, Gohra would have enemies on both sides. Even if there was no alliance with the Sem, all it would take is a poorly timed invasion, such as the attack on Stafolos, to deal a hard blow to an undefended Mongaul. Still—"

"Yes?"

"The Mongauli host that Siba and I spied from the ridge was no last-minute gathering in response to the attack on Stafolos. The scale was far too great for that. The bridge across the Kes was quickly built, but very strong and wide, and the soldiers were building a stronghold on this side of the river. Smoke rose from the forest roads that lead to Alvon, Talos and Tauride, and I can only guess that there were many messengers and a supply line, set to support their host for many days, weeks even.

"This was no host that could be assembled in one day and night!" Guin continued. "But why? Why would they assail Nospherus now? Mongaul has defeated Parros; they are at the pinnacle of victory. Normally this would call for a strengthening of their hold on the crystal city. They must organize their occupational forces, hunt out the remaining Parros loyalists. This would be the time for such things..."

"Know too that the invasion army is being led by none other than the Lady Amnelis, right hand of Archduke Vlad! She should be the one overseeing the occupation of Parros. It was her white knights that led the invasion!

"Why would she leave the job half done and turn her back on Parros for the invasion of Nospherus? There must be some other, greater reason, something to make the conquering of Nospherus a necessity for the armies of Mongaul."

Guin held his chin in his hand, turning possibilities over in his mind. "I do not understand—what is in Nospherus? What secret does this no-man's-land hold, for Mongaul to be driven to this?"

Loto and the Raku warriors huddled nearby said nothing, as if afraid to interrupt the thoughts of the great leopard-headed warrior. Half of what Guin said had no meaning for Loto or the others, but all the Sem who were present sensed from his speech that Mongaul's latest campaign posed an unprecedented threat to their future. Even as they talked, the vanguard of the Mongauli host might be moving into the hills like a slow but inexorable tidal wave, searching for the Raku village. The wildlings' fur-covered faces were clouded and set with tension. For the first time, they realized the severity of their situation.

Guin sat deep in thought for a while. Then, as though he had just noticed that the Sem were waiting for him to speak, he lifted his golden head and looked at Loto. "Regardless of their reasons," he said, his voice more forceful, "we must deal with the situation at once. The Mongauli have invaded in earnest. Not one of the Sem tribes, not the Raku, Karoi, or Guro, would stand a chance if it were to fight the Mongauli host on its own. Worse, from where the Mongauli crossed the Kes, this is the first Sem holding. Unless the Mongauli are unusually lucky, it will take them several days to find this village without maps or guides, hidden as it is in this valley; yet we cannot hope for such luck that they will miss the village entirely and proceed into inner Nospherus, leaving us in peace."

Guin paused, still looking at Loto. "The Mongauli are ten-and-five thousand, and all the able-bodied fighters of the Raku together are only two thousand. We could flee deeper into Nospherus, or burst out of these mountains and fight them here—but either path would be futile. All that is left to us—"

"But, Riyaad..." interrupted Loto, the shadow of fear dimming the sparkle of intelligence in his eyes. He shook his head as though he meant to say something but did not open his mouth again.

"We should leave the village now, escape!" One of the lesser chieftains standing along the wall behind Loto suddenly came forward. "It is the only way! The painted demons ride horses, they have weapons that hurl stones great distances!"

"Rinno!" shouted Loto, sternly scolding the younger Raku.

But Rinno would not stop. "Also, what Riyaad suggests, this is very, very impossible. The Raku cannot join forces with the Karoi, nor shall we fight alongside the detestable Guro. The Guro capture our folk and eat them alive! They eat our flesh, even though we are both Sem! And the Karoi, how many of our women and children have they stolen and made into slaves?"

"That is not all!" another lesser chieftain exclaimed. "The Karoi are only two thousand strong, and the Guro about the same. Even with the Rasa, the Tubai, and all the smaller tribes on top, we would not come close to matching the Mongauli demons in number!"

"Who are you?" Guin asked, turning to look at the new speaker.

"Ebu," the Raku stammered in reply. "I am Ebu, Riyaad."

"Now, Ebu—you, too, Rinno, and the rest of you—listen. I have been thinking upon this a long while. On the way here, the warriors who accompanied me told me of the friction between the tribes. Also I know that if all of them gathered, there would still be no more than seven thousand Sem, or perhaps eight at best. Our disadvantages are many: we have no pellet bows, nor horses; Sem warriors are but half the height of the shortest Mongauli; and we cannot say for certain if the current invasion force of ten-and-five thousand is truly the entire army. Since they have gone through the trouble of setting up supply lines and a base camp on this side of the Kes, we can probably assume that they have ten to twenty thousand more troops ready as backup. However—"

"We are doomed," shouted a voice of angry desperation from among the lesser chieftains.

"The Raku are finished," another chimed in.

"We will become slaves of the demons!"

"It is over."

Loto craned his neck to see who was speaking, ready to

chastise, but a high voice spoke before he could get the words out.

"We must fly! We must leave the village and hide the women, children, and the aged in the mountains."

"Sebu!"

"What else can we do?!" The Raku called Sebu stared around wildly at the others. "That is the only way we can escape death. Let us go north, to the mountains. Yes, we will cross the Dog's Head to Ashgarn in the north."

All at once the Sem clamored, their voices shouting in agreement with Sebu. Guin looked them over. Every face was filled with confusion, distrust, and fear. They were ready to begin their flight there and then—to gather all the food they could carry and leave their homes behind, setting out into the night for the unknown dangers of the north.

"Listen, please," said Guin, rising up and moving forward, but a loud "No!" from the back of the crowd stopped him.

A young Sem was shouting to be heard above the others. "We should fight first! If we lose, it will still not be too late to escape to the north!"

"What?" Sebu snarled, turning around. "Ah, it is you, Siba!" The lesser chieftain scowled and thrust his finger at the ground. "Sit. This is not the place for the outbursts of youths. This is a meeting of chieftains."

"What would you do once we went north?" continued Siba, undaunted. "Would you wait for the Mongauli demons to lose interest and give up? What would you do if they built a fortress here, in our valley? We would never be able to return!"

"They will not stay in Nospherus long. We will only have to wait a winter for them to give up and leave."

"But there is no food in the northern mountains. What if the Mongauli set up camp here and followed with an attack on us in the mountains? Then, truly, it would be the end for the Raku."

"What difference does it make? We cannot fight them and win," Sebu declared with finality.

Seeing Siba ready to reply again, Loto stood up slowly. Spreading his arms, he quieted the two. "There is no time for this quarrelling."

"Indeed," Guin added in a low growl. "We have precious little time, and much to decide. Now, listen. I have an idea."

Loto, Siba, Sebu, Ebu, Rinno, and the twenty or so other Raku leaders gathered there all fixed their eyes on the leopard-headed man who now loomed above them in the half light of the firepit.

"I suggest—" Guin began slowly, measuring his words, but a commotion near the hut's entrance cut him off. A young Raku warrior pushed his way between the chieftains standing there.

Bowing quickly to them, he turned to Loto and Guin.

"The chiefs of the Tubai and Rasa head this way. They will be at the entrance to the valley shortly."

"That was quick," Guin observed.

Loto nodded. "The Tubai and Rasa are close to the Raku. The Rasa have a village on the mountain that rises above this valley."

"This hut is too small for our meeting, now," Guin declared loudly. "Let us move to the clearing, where we can speak not only to the chieftains, but to all of the Raku. Outside!"

The Raku chieftains nodded and began to move toward the exit. Siba stayed close to Guin, looking up at him with concern in his eyes. He nodded to the leopard-man as if to beseech him not to worry.

Guin's voice came in a low growl through his feline mask. "The Tubai and the Rasa are here…the Karoi and Guro are the problem. Will they join forces with the Raku…?"

"Riyaad?" said Siba.

Guin shook his head. Bending low, he stepped out of the hut into the cool night air.

───── 2 ─────

While the leopard-headed warrior was engaged in deliber-
ations with Loto and his chiefs about how to meet the
oncoming invasion army, Rinda, Remus, the faithful Suni,
and the mercenary Istavan were enjoying the feast in the
women's house across the clearing.

It seemed that the two large huts on either side of the central clearing were the only communal buildings in the village.
On the west was the chieftain's hut where matters concerning
the village were debated, and across from it on the east was the
feasting hut, where guests were greeted and food was prepared.
Guin had been rushed to the council of war without so much as
a moment's rest, but in the cheerful space he left behind, the
Raku women were fussing and bustling to and fro to entertain
their unusual guests.

The hut that Istavan and the twins had been welcomed into
was much the same as the one Guin had entered later. The

floor was hollowed out, with a fire pit dug at the center. Around the pit lay dried rushes and comfortable-looking sun-bleached skins to sit on. A great feast continued to be laid out before the visitors, one hearty dish after another, accompanied by jugs of wine and milk.

Istavan sat on a pile of skins, his legs folded in the Valachian fashion, and his black eyes sparkled as he watched the Sem women work. By rights, he should have been in the other hut with Guin, planning their strategy against the Mongauli, but Istavan Spellsword was not one to be overly concerned about things that did not concern him—and besides, he was hungry, and his throat was parched. Despite his considerable battlefield experience, the young mercenary was still more of a child than a full-fledged warrior.

He sat in the light of the fire, relaxing. Although he remained self-conscious about his disheveled appearance, he eagerly examined the feast being laid out before him, wondering just how much would come, and how good it would taste.

"Not that we can expect much from these monkeys, eh?" Istavan declared in a loud voice, knowing it would irk the twins. "Who knows what they're feeding us! The monkeys of Nospherus gobble down some pretty peculiar things: the moss that clings to the underside of wildlands rocks, slippery earth eaters...I'm sure that's what they expect us to eat! Ach, and by the by, how it stinks of monkey in here!"

Rinda couldn't stop herself from snapping back at him, though she knew how pleased the mercenary would be to see her upset. "How can you say such things, with all they're doing for us? What if they understood you? And the Raku are *not* monkeys! They are very kind, and gentle, and caring—far more human than you or any of those Gohran demons who used to be your comrades, Istavan of Valachia!"

"You seem awfully fond of the little buggers! Maybe you're related, eh? Got a monkey for a grandfather? A baboon climb up your family tree somewhere?" the mercenary teased, his dark eyes flashing.

"You would slander the royal family of Parros?!" Rinda spluttered, furious.

"Stop paying him attention, Rinda. He'll just try to annoy us more," advised Remus.

"Ah, stop your chittering, you're the biggest monkey of them all, kid!" Istavan laughed, shooting Remus an exaggerated glare. But then a large, glazed pot was set before him, into which he immediately dipped his hand. Liking his first mouthful of the pot's contents, he disregarded the twins entirely for the next few moments.

"Hrmm," the mercenary made a pleased noise, his mouth stuffed full of food. "Not bad, not bad at all." He swallowed the food with evident relish. "Berries from the rock amaranth, I'd say—steamed in horsemilk? This is tasty! Those monkeys really went all out. Hey, here—try some!"

"We've had our fill, thank you," replied Rinda with a sly smile, pushing the dish back toward the mercenary. "We've been in the Raku village, eating and resting while you and Guin were losing the Mongauli army in the wildlands. You must be very tired, Istavan. We thank you for your courage."

The mercenary was startled at the unexpected nod of gratitude from Rinda. He stole a quick look over at the princess, but her sly smile had melted and in its place was the innocent face of a cherub who would not harm a fly, let alone speak an unkind or veiled word. Remus stuck his face in his jug, drinking milk in gulps.

"Good eating, this," Istavan proclaimed, turning back to his food. The Raku women pushed more plates towards him. They had prepared a true feast for their guests, making the most out of what little edibles the wastes of Nospherus had to offer. There was a thick, green soup of rockmoss, and fried mushrooms of a kind that Istavan had seen growing in the wildland rocks' nooks and crannies, where moisture gathered in the mornings. There were baked sand lizards, succulent peeled cactus fruits, and amaranth dumplings. Istavan licked his lips and whistled in astonishment at the variety.

The Raku women apparently thought they had thirty visitors, not three, for they kept bringing dish after dish piled high with food. Sem children played at the women's feet and gazed up at the plates with wide, hungry eyes, but all they received was a slap on the temple and a push towards the door.

Istavan paid them no mind as he hungrily munched on juicy cactus pulp and dipped amaranth dumplings in stew. He crammed them into his mouth two at a time, entirely forgetting all the misgivings he had proclaimed to have about smelly monkey food. Suni sat at Rinda's feet, leaning against the girl's legs, and looked accusingly at the mercenary's busy mouth.

"Mmm, this one's good, too. Wonder how I made it this far on vasya berries?" Istavan grimaced. "That reminds me. Once, on the Corsea, the ship I was sailing on got wrecked, and I was forced to eat a shipmate so I wouldn't starve—don't tell anyone about this, you hear? I've got confidence enough in my ability to survive, no matter what the circumstances, however fate handles me. But I'm happy to say that was the only time I ever considered cutting off my own leg and eating it!"

"You certainly have had some remarkable adventures, young as you may be," purred Rinda, smiling and tilting her head endearingly. A day's rest had done her good; a youthful sparkle had come back to her eyes and a healthy glow had returned to her skin. She had bathed for the first time in what

seemed like ages, and combed her hair, becoming once again a fairy-like young girl. In the darkness of the hut, she and her brother were beams of moonlight. They were full of life and noble beauty.

Suni's eyes had returned to the twins, where they were fixed in a reverent gaze. Istavan noticed and was on the verge of making some malicious remark but changed his mind. He looked up at Rinda and smiled.

"Yes," said the mercenary, dripping with pride, "I've had just about any experience you can think of. I am the Crimson Mercenary, after all—Istavan of Valachia! Never stumped no matter what I run into, cutting through anything that gets in my way. What's more, I'm different from your average hero—I've got a destiny, I have. Why, sometimes I impress even myself, I wonder just how far I'll go! Ah, but I do love adventure!"

"And yourself, it sounds like," added Remus, giggling.

But Istavan refused to be put off and continued with undiminished enthusiasm. "I'll be a king before you know it, believe you me! Or emperor, even—anything's possible for me! Yeah, my beginnings may have been humble, but I'll show the world that I mean business. I'm not like others. I can sense danger, you see, and slip out of the tightest spots with flair—the stars are on my side, now and for always! And by the pale light of Aeris, mark my words: when I meet the Shining Lady, the path to my throne, and to my destiny, will open wide before me.

"How about it, little princess? Maybe I've already met my Shining Lady, eh? I mean, look at the way the firelight makes your hair glow all over with silver, and your eyes shine like you were a doll made of stardust and moonlight. I wonder, did I mention...yes I must have, but I'll say it again. You really are quite beautiful!" Having said this Istavan cackled drunkenly and slammed his empty jug down on the table before him. One of the serving women quickly approached and refilled his jug with wine.

"Watch what you say to my sister," Remus warned, his temper rising. But Rinda laughed warmly, and patted her brother on the shoulder.

"Why, thank you for your most kind words, Istavan of Valachia. But really, the food is getting cold. We mustn't let the Raku's generous feast go to waste! Here, try this, it's very good!"

"I believe I shall! I certainly shan't disregard the advice of my queen bride to be!"

Istavan reached out to take the plate that Rinda offered him. Upon it was something whitish and translucent save that half of it which was scorched black by a cooking fire. It was not very pleasant to the eye, and for a moment as he reached for it Istavan wondered in the back of his mind what it was. But he was too caught up in his own merry mood to notice the concern on the faces of the Raku women, and the way that the twins exchanged conspiratorial glances and jabbed each other in the ribs, barely holding back laughter. With his right hand he picked up a slimy chunk of the stuff, stuffed it in his mouth, and chewed slowly, three times.

His face twisted with revulsion. Spitting his slimy mouthful onto the ground, he yelled, "What in Doal's name—?" His tanned face turned a dark red.

Rinda and Remus burst into laughter, slapping their thighs and doubling over in their mirth. The Raku women hurried toward them, making startled gestures.

"They fear," Rinda interpreted through sobs of laughter, "that it did not meet milord's liking!"

"Meet my liking? Gaah! What is that thing?"

"Why, exactly what you ordered, Istavan: baked sand leech!" Rinda's laugh was so loud that she startled Suni up from where she was sitting at the princess's feet.

"S-Sand leech?!" The mercenary's eyes went round, and he spat again on the dirt floor. "Peh!" He looked on the verge of vomiting. "When did I ever ask for it?"

"Don't you remember saying, 'They better have a black pig roast, or a sand leech roast at least waiting for us'? Why, the kind Raku were only trying to please you!"

"Indeed," Remus added, "they asked us many times if the

dark-skinned one really ate sand leeches! 'Do they eat sand leeches in his country? It is forbidden among our people, for they feed upon the corpses of the dead!'" Remus made a face like a concerned Raku matron, and then slapped his hand over his mouth to stifle a peal of laughter that brought tears to his eyes.

Istavan's stomach churned, and he hopped lightly away from the lump of sand leech flesh on the ground, as though it were poised to leap up and attack him at any moment. This sent the twins into another bout of laughter, further irking the flustered mercenary.

"Brats! Churls! Have your fun with me, will you? I see now, you had it planned all along! You were smiling much too sweetly, I ought've guessed! Miserable wretches!" Istavan's tightly drawn cheeks turned bright red as he swore at the twins of Parros. "Heed my words, accursed twins! By the eight crotches of Doal's nine tails, I've saved your tainted hides for the last time. By the slimy dung of Doal's black swine, and the three hag sisters born from it, you'll pay for this! Aye, you'll pay!"

"But," said Rinda, her face as innocent as a kitten's, "you *did* ask to eat the sand leech, did you not? Why, it's quite rude of you to suggest that we were plotting against you. Aren't you the Spellsword Istavan, who can sense danger and is never surprised come what may?"

Istavan was out of his mind now. He lunged and tried to

grab the twins, who laughed and jumped nimbly away, leaving poor Suni to tumble squealing across the ground. The Raku women hurried up from all directions, waving their arms in an attempt to calm the raging mercenary.

"Wait!"

Rinda stopped abruptly, straining to listen to a noise coming from outside the hut. Voices, Sem voices, were arguing loudly. A look of worry came over Rinda's face and she turned to her brother. "Remus?"

Remus looked at his sister, then went to the doorway to see what was going on outside. He quickly ran back into the hut, cheeks puffed with excitement. "It's the Sem! They're all out there!"

"What?" exclaimed Istavan, swiftly recovering his sword from where he had cast it on the ground and heading out the doorway. Rinda, Remus, and Suni followed close after him...then stopped in their tracks.

A great crowd, no, an army of Sem had gathered in the clearing at the center of the village, filling the place up, spilling out between the huts around it; probably their numbers stretched all the way to the village gate. It was hard to see in the torchlight, but Istavan thought there had to be two or three thousand of the ape-like warriors there, a vast throng composed of many smaller bands and irregular clusters. Chieftains stood at the head of each group, all jostling for space in the crowded clearing.

The torches set around the clearing were reflected in the Sem's eyes, which shone like innumerable stars in an inverted sky. The axes in their hands and the arrows in their quivers floated around them, pale white in the flickering firelight. All the faces were turned up towards a pedestal in the middle of the throng. Upon it stood Guin, towering over all in the clearing. He noticed Istavan and the twins and gave them a curt nod. Then, in a great voice, he called out for the chieftains to approach the pedestal. He asked the other warriors to sit down and for the ubiquitous Raku children to be sent out of the crowd and into their homes.

Thus began the meeting of the tribes.

—— 3 ——

It was a night that would long remain vivid in the memories of all who were there. For Rinda and Remus, in particular, it was the true beginning of an adventure that would surpass all of the strange and wonderful things they had experienced since their first encounter with the leopard-headed warrior Guin.

Rinda held her brother's hand as she sat on her knees at the entrance of the house into which the twins had been welcomed; the faithful Suni was curled quietly in the doorway behind her. The naughty princess who had teased Istavan a few moments ago was gone. Rinda's violet eyes were meditative now as she silently surveyed the crowds of Sem thronging in the clearing before her.

She could sense the trepidation in the air. Everyone and everything in the village seemed suffused by fear of a future that none could foresee. She shuddered. The heavy air of destiny that filled the night was tangible to her, and she sensed the strength and desperation of the Sem people's desire to live. She breathed deeply and tried to calm herself. Her mind drifted to her own predicament, and in a flood, the weight of the last few days came crushing down onto her, with all of the changes those days had brought. She wept.

Parros glimmered in her mind's eye. Had she truly walked down those royal corridors? Parros, the ancient kingdom, flourishing and perfect, flower of the Middle Country—at its center the Crystal Palace, the gem in the royal crown. And in that crown had been set two pearls, Rinda and Remus, the twins of Parros, so well protected that not even a stray breeze was allowed to touch them. Rinda had thought her charmed life perfect, and eternal.

But it was gone. Not in their wildest dreams had the lords of Parros imagined that the holy kingdom might be attacked across its northern border, where there had been peace for so many years. But attacked it had been; and it did not take three days for the shields of Parros to falter and the Crystal Palace to fall. The young prince and princess watched as their lord father and lady mother were cut down where they sat on the jeweled thrones of the burning palace, their blood let to run in streams in their own court.

Images flooded through Rinda's mind: their nursemaid Boganne's tears as she fled with them down through the ancient halls; Minister Riya and the mysterious ancient machinery to which they were brought. If that strange artifact had sent them where it was supposed to—to Earlgos, where their aunt was queen—things would have been much different. But the hands of fate had moved again, sending the twins—and with them, the hope that Parros would someday rise again—tumbling onto the forest floor in the Roodwood. The cruelty of it! Stuck in the middle of Mongaul, one of the three archduchies of their enemy Gohra that had destroyed Parros. But it was in the Roodwood that they had met Guin, and he had protected them from the ghouls of the Marches forest, freed them from the cells of Stafolos Keep, and guarded them during the siege that had destroyed that fortress. Rinda shook her head as she remembered the Sem warriors crowding those narrow halls, the screams, the smoke, and the blood...so much blood.

Fate's skein is twisted, thought the princess, snuggling closer to her brother. *I know not where it will lead us next...but one thing I do know. These last several days have been like ten years spent in the halls of the Crystal Palace. So filled with adventure and excitement I've hardly had time to catch my breath!* Remembering the gentle color and beauty of her lost home, Rinda sighed. She and her brother had been the love of all. And now, every day seemed like her last left to live!

Yet—here they were, the Pearls of Parros, alive and unscathed. *Sweet god Janos, we thank you from our hearts!* thought Rinda, putting one slender hand on her breast. She already knew, deep inside, that the constant trials and rapid pace of adventure had changed her and her brother greatly. No longer were they the two children who had clung together so desperately in the vasya bushes of the Roodwood, crying helplessly. Here in the no-man's-land, their future entrusted to a barbarian race, they sat untrembling as that alien people's fate began to unfold.

Surely, if some seer back in the marbled halls of the Crystal Palace had prophesied that such events as these would come to pass, he would have been mocked out of court as a fraud. But it had all really happened, and there to prove it were the Pearls.

We're so far from Parros, so horribly far, thought Rinda, wondering if she would ever see something as beautiful as the shining towers of the Crystal Palace again, the spires that had burned and fallen before her eyes. Her hatred for the Mongauli who had killed her father and mother and trampled the beautiful city beneath their hooves had not waned in the least. Instead, it had been transformed, over the past few terrible days, into something hard, a crystalline will for revenge that nothing could erode. She would not waste away grieving for the lost idyll of her buried home. She was too young and full of life for that, and in fact, she felt alive more than anything else now.

As it is with most spirited children, the twins loved adventure. New sights and thrilling scenes stole their hearts. What

Rinda and Remus had experienced over the past few days was far more remarkable than anything they had ever seen or imagined, sheltered as they had been in the beautiful halls and courtyards behind the palace walls. Dreadful as their journey had been, it had also opened their minds and filled them with the excitement of exploration.

And then there was Guin...

Rinda clutched Remus's hand tightly, feeling its warmth in her own, and turned her eyes to look at that amazing god of a man. She was struck again by the power of his presence. He was standing atop the high stone pedestal in the middle of the clearing, with Loto and the other Raku chieftains arrayed on either side; he cast a fierce gaze over the gathered Sem, describing the approaching Mongauli army and the dire threat that faced them all. To Rinda, whose understanding of the Sem tongue had not progressed much beyond communicating with Suni via hand gestures and facial expressions, the words of Guin's impassioned speech were gibberish. But the quality of his voice and the way he held the crowd was such that her ignorance of the Sem language did not tarnish the impact of the scene.

The only space in the clearing not packed full with wildling troops was a small circle surrounding the jutting rock that served as Guin's pedestal. Within this circle the elders and tribal chieftains sat. They wore painted feathers in their hair, and their bodies were wrapped in long fur cloaks; their bushy eyebrows were graying, and some of the eldest had gone white with age. Behind the old chieftains stood standard-bearers holding up spears with flags that marked the divisions of the armies of each tribe. Each of them was accompanied by a few warriors in charge of looking after their respective flag; behind them, the rest of the warriors sat in tightly packed rows. This was more than enough to fill the central clearing, and the tail end of each row spread out between the houses, in some places half-pushing through the doorways into the homes of the Raku.

All told, the Sem numbers in the village had swollen to almost five thousand, covering the entire end of the valley in a thick, furry blanket. Though not unheard of, it was rare for such a large number of Sem to gather in one place. High Chieftain Loto had sent a call for all able warriors to the neighboring Rasa and Tubai villages, and among the Sem, warriors included women and children, who picked up weapons and fought alongside the men, often with equal skill in battle. Among the Sem, the only ones who did not fight were those so aged that they could not move, and infants still at their mother's breasts.

Moreover, when they came, the Rasa and the Tubai had brought not only their warriors, but also their elderly and women with infant children. Unable to find room within the already crowded village, the non-combatants had spread to fill every available space in the surrounding valley. They were packed in so tightly that there was scarcely room to breathe. They pushed against each other, jostling to get closer to the central clearing to catch a glimpse of the strange warrior who had summoned them and to hear what their leaders were discussing.

In the clearing, all ears were perked, listening. They had already heard of the Mongauli invasion, and they knew that this was by far the largest force that had ever been unleashed upon the wildlings of Nospherus. Unless the invaders could somehow be turned back, it was certain that all the tribes would be demolished. The faces of the Sem were set in hard lines and not a voice was heard among the crowd. Even the children kept silent, sensing that this was not a time for play.

All eyes were fixed on the bizarre visitor, the great half-man, half-leopard warrior who towered above them now. Guin had been introduced to them by the high chieftain as the very son of Alphetto, the Sem god of war. But even without such an introduction, they would have known that Guin was no mere human. Among the diminutive wildlings the leopard-man stood incredibly tall, and his presence was overwhelming. It was as if he were not a man at all, but a statue of some divine being at whose feet the Sem had come to worship.

The firelight lit his bare torso, casting rippled shadows across the muscles of his chest, and the glow of the light on his giant leopard head seemed to threaten the very darkness around it. He was no ordinary warrior—or even hero—but a demigod sent to lead the Sem truly into the battle that would determine their fate. He was the messenger of that fate, and surely, if they followed his counsel, he would as their war-god lead them to victory. This was what the women gathered there said in soft whispers.

Guin knew nothing of this as he continued in his passionate attempt to convince the tribal chieftains that they must join battle together against the Gohrans.

"Of course, the Rasa are willing to fight, but we are not fools!" said Kalto, the leader of the Rasa. Befitting his tribe's nickname of "spotfur," his body was covered in fur of mottled black and gray, giving his rather large figure a humorous and gentle look belied by the bile in his words. "The Rasa do not wish to fight a battle that cannot be won!"

"It can be won!" declared Guin, sending gasps through the crowd. "I swear we have a chance. But to do this, all the Sem must move as one. One mind, one strength!"

"You speak of joining with the Guro and the Karoi, but this we cannot do!" shouted one of the Tubai chieftains. "The Karoi are the enemies of the Tubai."

"The Karoi and the Guro would not give their aid to the Raku and the Rasa!" shouted another. "They call the Raku weak, they make jest of us!"

"This is true, Riyaad," said Siba. Siba stood with his troops right behind Guin, as an honor guard of sorts, and occasionally he would whisper the names and standings of the speakers to Guin.

"Gaulo, the high chieftain of the Karoi, and Ilateli of the Guro both mock us," the Tubai chieftain explained. "They say that the Raku are like war-fearing women."

"But if we do not have the Karoi and Guro," the other chieftain went on, "then all the Raku and the Rasa and the Tubai put together, women and children included, cannot match the *oh-mu*." Behind Guin, Siba whispered that *oh-mu*, meaning "hairless ones," was the Sem word for humans.

"But to wait here is to wait for our own deaths!" came a voice from the Raku. The Raku chieftains had already heard Guin speak in the meeting hut, and many of them agreed with him that meeting their enemies offered their only hope of survival. "Can we trust that the demons will give up if we leave our villages and homes to hide in the mountains? What if they follow us and hunt us down? Then we are finished."

"No!" the Tubai chieftain shouted. "The Rasa and Tubai should come hide here in the Raku valley and wait for the *oh-mu* to pass!" Many furred heads nodded in agreement.

"That is poor counsel," Loto declared, his voice rising clear and loud. Silence came over the crowd, and all turned their heads to listen. "If by some chance a patrol found our valley, we would be lost. And we must consider the Karoi and Guro. The valleys where they live are easier to find than ours. Even if they are our enemies, we cannot abandon them as prey for the *oh-mu*."

"The *oh-mu* would surely torture any captives they take," pointed out the Raku chief Rinno, "and thus they would find our village."

"High chieftain! Have you sent messengers to the Karoi and the Guro?" asked the high chieftain of the Tubai.

"Yes, Tubai of the Tubai," Loto answered calmly. "I sent them out with the messengers who went to your village and to that of the Rasa. They should return with an answer soon."

"If they have not been eaten by our would-be allies!" spat Tubai. He was extremely large for a Sem, nearly as tall as Remus in height, but more striking was his face and tail. His face wore a white scar in the shape of a slanted cross, the relic of some great battle of old, while his tail had been severed near the base, leaving nothing but a scarred stump. "Even if they are not eaten, and we make our pleas heard, with our heads bowed low, it does not mean that the Karoi or the Guro will come to our aid."

"Wait! Listen to me!" Guin shouted, pacing back and forth on the flat top of the rocky pedestal. He beat his chest with a sound like sudden thunder, and immediately the chittering among the Sem died down, and they turned to listen to him once more. His voice was commanding. "Listen to what I have to say, brave Sem. While we waste time debating, the Mongauli army moves deeper into Nospherus! I do not know if the Karoi will come, or if the Guro will aid us. I do not know how long we can stand against the Mongauli with just the tribes gathered here. But being outnumbered is not cause to abandon hope! Miracles do happen!" Guin now had the undivided attention of the crowd. "There is one thing of which you may be sure: if we sit here letting time slip past us, there will be no miracle. The Mongauli army will come here to this valley with their soldiers and annihilate you."

Guin paused and looked over the gathered warriors. Then he spoke again, his voice steady and loud enough to carry to the far edges of the village.

"I say we have no time for debate. Indeed, we have no need for it, since the decision has been made for us. We must fight. There is no other path!"

"Riyaad!" Sebu stood up fearfully and shouted to be heard above the cheers that rose in response to Guin's speech. "Riyaad, you said there is a way we can win. But how can we, who are lesser in number, lesser in height, and lesser in arms, hope to win against the *oh-mu*?"

Shouts of agreement came from the crowd. Guin raised his hand for silence.

"One factor gives us a chance to win," said the leopard-headed warrior with confidence. "And I only need one word to explain it...Nospherus!"

The Sem exchanged confused glances. Guin was about to begin his explanation when there was a great commotion at the valley entrance.

"What is it?" demanded Loto, standing up. Siba sprang into the crowd and began pushing his way toward the source of the commotion to see what the matter was, but shouts reported the news before he had gone far.

"Guro! The Guro have come!"

Shouts of surprise, then cheers of joy came from the crowds near the gate.

"What?" Startled, Loto craned his neck toward the mouth of the valley, trying to see over the thronging warriors. Just then, the tightly packed crowds of women and children on the main road parted in two, opening a path to the clearing. There were shouts of "Guro!" and "Ilateli!" and exuberant war cries from the Sem already gathered.

And so, in four even columns, the Guro warriors marched

wordlessly into the valley of the Raku, showered by cheers and shouts of joy.

"What's this?" said Siba, tears in his eyes as he looked toward Guin. "The proud, black-haired Guro have come to our village, the valley of the Raku whom they call brownhairs and fools... Their great chieftain himself leads them!"

"Siba, there was nothing to worry about," Guin said in a low voice. "I knew they would come. No matter how much the Guro look down on the Raku, or how much your two tribes quarrel, the Guro know they cannot face the Mongauli alone. When they heard the message from Loto's runners, and the scouts they sent out verified it, they had no choice but to forget all posturing and ill-will between you and come here."

"Riyaad..." breathed Siba, overcome with emotion.

Guin laughed. "I was only worried that they would spend too long trying to decide, and the Mongauli army would come too close for us to act. Thankfully, the Guro moved much more swiftly than I had imagined. This greatly increases our chances of winning."

Siba nodded.

By this time the Guro warriors, still being hailed with shouts of joy, had reached the central clearing. Of the Nospherus Sem, they were the second most numerous after the Raku, and, as their nickname, the "blackhairs," implied, their hair was darker than that of the other wildlings. The Guro made their home deeper in Nospherus than the valley of the Raku, in the desert where only rocks and small shrubs grew, so they did not adorn themselves with feathers. Instead they wrapped their bodies in the ominously colored skins of lizards. Among the Guro, the hide of a lizard was the mark of a warrior.

At their head was the one they called the great chieftain, Ilateli. He stood as tall as Tubai of the Tubai, and his black hair was exceptionally long and thick. His face was covered with a pattern of strikingly colorful warpaints. His greeting to Loto was somewhat taciturn, but they exchanged a friendly embrace, and then, as was the custom, he thrust out a spear towards Loto with a sand lizard impaled on its tip, an offering of friendship to a comrade in battle.

The warriors of the Guro tribe that followed after him all looked as though they were each match enough for a hundred foes, but they were far fewer in number than Guin had expected. The reason came directly from Ilateli's mouth.

"I thought that if all my warriors came into the valley along with the Tubai and the Rasa, the valley of the Raku would fill with more Sem than the Kes has *riyolaat*," he said. "The women and children of the Guro, too, are warriors, and they would not fit into this place. That is why I have only brought my chieftains and my strongest warriors here. The rest wait outside the valley. If there is need, they are all ready to come here at once."

"Thank you, Ilateli," said Loto, clasping his new friend in a heartfelt embrace. Tubai of the Tubai and Kalto of the Rasa joined Loto in welcoming the Guro leader. But the Guro chieftain had already noticed Guin. He looked at the leopard-headed warrior with naked disbelief, half in fear and half in awe of this giant among them. Loto explained Guin's role, and told Ilateli what he had said to them, and it seemed the leader of the Guro was even more taken with this otherworldly warrior.

"But what is the meaning of this?" asked Ilateli after the cries of welcome had died down, and he had the attention of all the chieftains. "You have called us with urgent cause, pulled us out of our bedskins, yet three tribes sit here on the ground without a drop of warpaint on your face, not a single arrowhead prepared!"

"We have been debating," Loto admitted, "whether to fight the painted *oh-mu* demons or to escape to the mountains in the north and wait for them to leave."

Ilateli angrily thrust the butt of his spear into the ground. "This is no time for discussion! As soon as we received your message, we sent scouts to where you said the *oh-mu* were coming from and saw there a great host of the painted demons. They are heading due east, and will find this village of the Raku in two days! Even now, in the Guro tents, the women and children dip arrows into the poison pots, and sharpen the spears and axes, for war is upon us!"

Murmuring rose up from the Sem, and Guin's eyes shone with a hard light. He had thought the Mongauli army would not risk a night march, but camp and wait for the sun to rise before moving. From what the Guro chieftain was saying, however, it seemed that the enemy had decided to shoulder the risks and march through the wastes of Nospherus in the darkness. Danger was not yet imminent, for the hills around the valley would conceal them from Mongauli eyes for a while. Yet there was no doubt that the Gohran army would send out scouts to explore the land before it as it proceeded deeper into Nospherus, and the valley of the Raku would eventually be found.

"To battle!"

The Raku warriors were the first to stand and give the cry.

"To battle!" echoed Guin, sounding relieved. He jumped down from the stone pedestal and nodded to Ilateli. The Sem warrior stood next to him, barely coming up to his waist, but he proudly stuck out his chest and returned the leopard-man's look of approval.

The sky to the east was slowly growing lighter. Morning had come to Nospherus, and with it, the first winds of the coming clash.

4

In moments, the valley of the Raku was a sea of furious activity. The warriors of the Guro, Rasa, and Tubai were the first to move out the valley. They gathered their troops according to tribe and awaited orders to march.

The Raku women raided their stores for all the food they could find, and for a while they were busy preparing and serving a meal for the warriors of the other tribes who had run through the night to attend the council and now were weary and in need of nourishment. It was also the women's job to gather the flowers from which the Sem drew the poison they used to make their poison arrows, the most fearsome weapon in the wildling arsenal. The Raku women mashed these flowers and strained the juice into small jars which were placed on the cooking fires to boil until the thin juices had become a viscous toxic brew. This they applied to the tips of innumerable arrows, which were then lined up to dry. Meanwhile, other women went around the camps, checking warriors' bows to see that they were not warped and that the bowstrings had not snapped. With skilled hands they mended the ones in need of repair. Still others went into the hills and gathered strange grasses from which they made essences for warding off the many poisonous serpents and sand leeches that made their home in Nospherus. They placed these hastily concocted essences into small leather pouches, which were distributed among the gathered warriors.

The warriors, for their part, prepared themselves for the coming battle. They ate and slept as they could, but most were kept busy sharpening their stone axes and boiling down a kind of red moss which they had gathered and kept dried in glazed jars. From the boiled moss they now made the ruddy brown pigment they would use to paint elaborate patterns on their faces to show that they were warriors and to drive fear into the hearts of their enemies. Meanwhile, the chieftains and other leaders among the Sem gathered in the chieftain's hut, where they deliberated over possible battle plans.

It was nothing like the peaceful Raku village in which Rinda, Remus, and Suni had arrived the day before.

Rinda offered to help the women of the village, using gestures to communicate her desire to Suni. The princess picked up a stone scoop to help mix the poison pots, but Suni and the Raku women would hear nothing of it. And so Rinda took her brother by the hand and found an out-of-the-way corner of the clearing in which they could sit and watch the bustling of the village as it prepared for war.

The night had given way to dawn and another dry, hot Nospherus day was beginning. In the early morning light, the twins could see the wildling warriors making ready for battle. The men of each tribe had painted their faces with different colors of war paint. They moved about the clearing, stone axes at their waists, weaving between the women who were carrying jars and bundles of arrows this way and that. Everywhere there was the endless chitter of Sem voices, the scent of things boiling, and the smell of wood fires. Guin had gone into the chieftain's hut, making arrangements and giving orders, and for a long time he did not show himself outside.

At first, the mercenary Istavan sat next to Rinda and Remus and grumbled about one thing or another, half-heartedly making fun of the Raku women hustling by. Soon, however, he decided that it would sully his image to be seen consorting with children, and so he made his way into the chieftain's hut and did not come back out.

The sound of hasty activity and the palpable tension in the air spread throughout the valley on the scurrying legs of the Sem. The twins saw one squad of Sem run into the clearing bearing flags that were no more than fur tassels strung on the ends of spears. Lowering these makeshift flags, they rushed into the chieftain's hut to receive their orders, then moments later came hurrying back out and disappeared up the road toward the mouth of the valley.

"Rinda," whispered Remus to his sister. His eyes were wide with boyish excitement at the warriors' preparations for battle. "Rinda, I never would have imagined we'd get to see this! Not in my wildest dreams!"

"Truly," his sister agreed. "Not in the Crystal Palace of Parros, not in the Marches wood, not in that cell in Stafolos Keep...not even last night, curled up on the floor in our hut, holding our breaths, waiting for Guin to come back. This is truly marvelous." She, too, was completely entranced by the goings-on.

"Rinda?"

"Yes?"

"What do you think will happen next?"

"I don't know. What will happen will happen, I suppose." Rinda was irritated by the question. "But I think that we are no longer two children without a country, on the run from the armies of our enemies." She paused, working up the courage to say something that had been on her mind ever since they had learned that they were going to fight. "Remus, I want to join Suni's band and fight the Mongauli, too!"

"I feel the same way, Rinda…but do you really think we can win?" he replied, gazing at the Sem running back and forth in front of them, his eyebrows wrinkled with worry.

"Of course we will!" Rinda exclaimed, irritated by her brother once again. "We've got Guin, Remus! Guin!!"

"But you heard what they said. There's so many of them! And they've got horses, too—"

"One more 'but' like that and I'll pull out that silly tongue of yours!" Rinda snapped, the girlish indignation making the blood rise in her cheeks. "We *will* win. We have to."

"Is that what you…feel?" Remus asked, in such a slow, careful way that for a moment, Rinda thought he was mocking her gift and gave him a withering glare.

What the princess had not yet realized was that the cautious manner she found so infuriating in her brother was the very essence of his character. It sprang from his utterly realistic way of viewing the world and his natural tendency to suspect before accepting anything. Though the twins looked nearly identical, their inner selves were as different as though the gods had played a game to see just how unlike they could make the two. Sensitive though she was, Rinda failed to recognize how different their personalities were, and so she was always irritated at what she regarded as her brother's failings. She often worried how she might make the coward she saw into a brave warrior, and someday, king—a task which she felt was her responsibility. Rinda had not yet realized that sometimes courage is the same thing as folly and that sometimes a skepticism bordering on cynicism is the best quality a king might hope to have. Perhaps her blindness to her brother's strengths was a result of her own sensitivity. She had lived her life aware of the realm of the gods, and this blinded her to some things in this world, including the depth of her brother's personality. She could not see how well he understood people, and how, ultimately, after he had gotten over his suspicions, he accepted them into his heart in a way that she could not.

"You mean did I 'see' us winning? The answer is no," she flared, scanning her brother's face for any trace of a jest. Finding none, she relaxed. "But we *do* have to win. We can't go back now. We can't retreat! If it comes to pass that the Sem are destroyed, then this land far from our home, this wasteland of Nospherus, will be where we make our last stand. If we let them capture us, Remus, they'll take us and drag us behind their horses again—this time to Torus, where they will kill us on the torturing block. They will cut off our heads and stick them atop the gates above the central market there."

Rinda shivered, scaring herself with her own words. "It's not that I fear death, Remus, it's just that I don't see that happening to us. We lived through the fall of Parros, and the fall of

Stafolos Keep, and I believe we survived thanks to our destiny. Yes, Remus, we bear a destiny! We must rebuild Parros. And—" Rinda grabbed her brother by the shoulder, drawing him nearer to her. "All will go well as long as we have Guin! Don't you think so? As long as he is with us, there is nothing we need fear. Our destiny will not let us die out here in Nospherus—I cannot think that. We, and Guin, are special. I know." She whispered the last, as though the words were an incantation.

"I don't know," Remus murmured. "I don't feel anything."

Deaf to the sadness in her brother's voice, Rinda continued, "Well I do! I am Rinda Farseer, and yes, I *do* feel something. Guin is not a normal person. No, and it's not because of his leopard head or because he's a great warrior. There is something more that separates Guin from all other people. You know what? I think it's because he has…a destiny."

"A destiny?"

"Yes," Rinda replied, sounding surer of herself by the moment. "Guin of course has a fated future like everyone else, but I mean something more than that. I think he has the power to change other people's destinies, wherever he goes! It's as if he is himself an embodiment of their destiny, too, or part of it—something like that." Rinda nodded, the force of her own words convincing her of their truth. "And that is what separates him from everyone else. That's what makes him special! Surely you must feel *that*, Remus! As long as Guin is on our side, there is nothing we need fear, and as long as he is here, the Mongauli army and these Sem wildlands are all just a step on the way to our own destiny."

Rinda's voice was filled with unmistakable excitement and a conviction that Remus knew would not easily be shaken. He squinted as he looked at her, as though she were bright as the sun. "I wish..." Remus began, his voice tinged with a deep, wounded pride, and envy, "I wish I could feel things, too..."

Rinda, heedless, gave her brother a sharp jab in the ribs with her elbow. "Look, Guin's come back out."

"I guess the meeting's done. I wonder if they're finally going to march." Remus craned his neck to see whether it looked like they were in a hurry.

"I'm sure of it," said Rinda.

The leaders of the Sem tribes surrounded Guin as he appeared in the entrance of the chieftain's hut like some giant instructor surrounded by his pupils. With the confidence of one born to lead, he gave orders to each chieftain. In awe, Rinda saw each bow reverently before rushing off to carry out his duties. "Watch, Remus—no matter how you look at him he is a born emperor. He is king, he is commander—he's a hero!" she declared, utterly enchanted.

Remus had turned his attention to a band of Sem that had

come down to the village center to give a report as the group of chiefs was leaving. "I wonder what news they have. They look like they've come in a terrible hurry."

"They're scouts returned from a patrol," answered Guin unexpectedly, walking towards them from the middle of the clearing. Remus jumped, startled.

"Guin! Is the war council done?" asked Rinda, rising to meet him.

Guin nodded slowly. "Did you rest well?" he asked, gazing up toward the entrance to the valley and placing a large hand atop each of the twins' heads.

"Yes, enough."

"Guin, when is the fighting going to start?"

"Soon—when I decide it shall begin," Guin replied. "Watch, the Raku warriors are leaving the valley."

It was as he said. The village clearing, so crowded only moments before, was nearly empty now. All the Sem warriors in their battle gear had hurried toward the mouth of the valley, where the army was now gathering, lining up by platoons.

"Guin?" asked Remus quietly. "Can we win?"

"I have been thinking," the leopard-headed warrior said, avoiding the question, "I have been wondering what to do with you two. The Sem of the Rasa, Raku, and Tubai are sending their aged and the women with children over the ridge, to

follow the spine of the hills toward the Dog's Head where they
have a place to hide. Soon, those of the Guro who will not be
fighting will join them. Already I have given the order for them
to come here and prepare for the journey. You could go with
them to the mountains. But then, should things go poorly, you
would be stuck out there." Guin scratched his furred chin.
"That said, we can't spare any to take you to Earlgos or such. We
have few enough fighters as it is."

"Why don't you ask us to fight?" Rinda accused angrily.
"We've just now decided never to leave your side again. Waiting
for you will be like torture, Guin! Give us weapons. We'll fight
by your side."

Guin shook his head. "I can understand why Mongaul is so
intent on finding the orphans of Parros," he muttered half to
himself. "If we had, right here, a way of understanding the trick
by which you were sent in an instant from Crystal to the middle
of the Roodwood, we could send you away from here, to a safer
place. If we only made that device bigger, we could send troops
wherever we want, whenever we want. No front would stand
against us; we could attack our enemies at our leisure, and
always catch them by surprise. Twins, you do not understand at
all how much they value you. You are worth far more than your
weight in gold, far more."

"But we have no idea how it works!" Rinda exclaimed.

"That artifact got us out here, yes—but we have no idea how, or why. Maybe if we had the Crystal Palace back, and the sealed temple—the Spire of Janos—we could learn. But now, we know so little about it." She spoke quickly, hoping her mind would stumble upon some bit of information that could help Guin.

Suddenly, Remus grabbed her arm.

"What?" his sister snapped.

"Rinda." The boy's voice had an echo of urgency in it.

She turned and looked in the direction he was looking just in time to see a dark face disappear quickly into the shadows beside the hut where they had feasted. She snapped her mouth shut and stuck out her lip in a pout.

"Coward! Eavesdropper!" the princess called out, casting a baleful gaze toward the shadow. But already the figure had vanished around the side of the hut.

"Ah, Guin—there you are," came a voice from behind them a few moments later. It was Istavan, his look of forced innocence marred by a smirk that suggested he might whistle up a jig at any moment. "This is no time to be chatting with the young 'uns! We've got to get going! The monkey army's all lined up waiting for their general."

"He's pretending he wasn't listening!" Rinda whispered to Remus.

Istavan grinned, ignoring the twins. "No matter how you

look at it, I don't think those Karoi are coming. By Ruah's fiery chariot, if they don't show up, we'll have to fight this war without them!"

"If that is the way it is, then so be it. We'll think of a way to wage this war," Guin answered.

"Right. Well, shall we get going?" The mercenary clapped Guin on the shoulder and turned to head off toward the valley entrance.

"But Guin, what about us? Where should we go?"

"You brats should stay here, with the monkey brats," the mercenary sneered.

"You'll take us with you, won't you?" Rinda asked Guin worriedly, ignoring Istavan.

"Time is precious." Guin sighed. "Children, come with me to the mouth of the valley. We will decide there."

"Yes!"

"Yes, Guin!"

The prince and princess had to walk fast to keep up with Guin. The last warriors had departed from the village of the Raku, and now the wildling army filled the broad slope of the valley mouth with painted faces and brandished spear-flags, all waiting for Guin. Siba came running up to escort the leopard-man, a troop of young Raku warriors behind him.

"Riyaad!"

"Yes, let us go." With the twins of Parros on either side and Istavan and Siba's band behind him, Guin headed up the slope from the village with giant strides. As the small band passed among the ranks of the army, cries went up from the warriors of the Raku, Guro, Tubai, and Rasa packed on both sides of the path.

The Sem warriors waved and pounded the hafts of their spears on the ground. "Riyaad! Riyaad!"

At the rear of the ranks, the elderly and the childbearing women, as well as the Raku women who would remain to protect the village, gathered and cheered, calling the names of their husbands and sons.

"Incredible! Look at all of them, look at the tribes!" whispered Rinda to her brother, gazing around with wide eyes. "Guin did all this in one day, Remus. Our Guin!"

"But the Mongauli have three times our number," replied her practical brother. "And the Karoi haven't showed up. That's a great loss. They're almost as many as the Guro, and even better fighters."

Rinda's expression changed to a look of gloom. "Blah! Don't say things to disappoint me." She scowled at the prince. "You're always like that... Say, where did Suni go?"

Remus shrugged and looked around. But he didn't have time to go hunting for Suni, for just then an outcry came from the vanguard of the army as it stood poised to leave the valley.

"What is it?" came Loto's shout.

"It's terrible—the messengers!"

"The messengers?" the chieftains murmured, and all craned their necks to see what the matter was.

From the head of the columns came a young Raku warrior, out of breath. He jostled his way through the ranks, and the Sem hurriedly stepped aside to let him through. He staggered and tumbled onto the ground in front of the Raku high chieftain.

"Nolu!" shouted Loto. The young warrior was covered with horrible wounds. There was a deep gash across his forehead, and the blood that ran from it had nearly blinded him, transforming his face into a crimson mask. His whole body was covered with cuts. The twins were amazed that he still breathed.

"He was one of the messengers we sent to the Karoi?" asked Guin.

"Yes, Riyaad."

"Th-The Karoi…" the messenger known as Nolu gasped. The Sem around them shouted when they saw what he held in his two hands.

Two heads, dripping blood.

"Gogu, and Ruki," Siba groaned. They were the two other messengers, warriors of the Raku, who had been sent to the Karoi with Nolu.

"Gaulo has this to say to Loto: 'The Karoi crossed the river and attacked the *oh-mu*, we are the brave warriors who burned down the castle. We do not need to join hands with the cowardly brownhairs or the yidoh-kin. The *oh-mu* fear the Karoi, they...they will part before us.'"

"Fools," spat Loto. "Someone, tend to Nolu."

Cries rose up from the assembled warriors:

"Cowards? They call us cowards?"

"It is the Karoi's fault the *oh-mu* crossed the river! They attacked them, they burned the *oh-mu* castle on the Kes!"

"Our enemy is the Karoi!"

There was a brief, tense silence when this was said. The silence was broken by more shouting from the ranks.

"Death to the Karoi!"

"Kill the Karoi!"

"Iiiya! Iiiya! Iiiya!"

A battle cry spread rapidly through the assembled army. All the Sem were standing, shouting and waving their spears and bows in the air.

Siba turned with a despairing look to Guin. "Riyaad!"

It was then that Guin rallied them.

"Wait, warriors of the Sem! Listen to me!" the piercing howl erupted from the leopard mask. And he began to address the Sem army.

Chapter Three

THE SECRET OF CAL MORU

I

In the pre-dawn hours of the same Nospherus morning on which the tribes of the Sem assembled for war, the Mongauli invaders were setting up camp in the vast wasteland of bleak and broken desert. Having crossed the Kes River two nights before and marched through the following day and night, they had finally been given orders to stop just as the false dawn was glimmering in the east. Wearily the Mongauli troops broke formation and spread out the thick woven blankets they carried in their packs and saddlebags. These would be their only bedding for the duration of the expedition. The cavalry gave the horses some of their precious water, and after the animals had been fed, the soldiers sat down to eat. Here and there grain balls were being kneaded, and dried meat was passed around. The only soldiers not resting were those on watch. They paced around the perimeter of the camp, crossbows in hand, watching in all directions across the vast wildlands.

From where the commanders had chosen to stop, nothing but rock and sand could be seen, all the way to the bumps of low mountains that marked the bland horizon. Crossing the Kes, the army had borne due east, and were it not still dark, they would have seen the Kanan Mountains farther eastward, while to the far north the lumps of the Ashgarns would have been visible, white beneath their eternal caps of snow. The Ashgarns seemed frightfully far away and mysterious on their march during the last day. The highest mountains the soldiers had ever seen, they were indeed the roof of the world. A considerable distance before the Kanan range, a few strangely shaped rocky crags stuck up from the desert, the only anchors for the eye in a vast sea of sand. These were the very same low, rocky mountains where the Sem tribes hid and made their villages—but this, of course, the Mongauli army did not know. Yet their commanders had given them orders to head straight for those mountains, and so they had done, like an iron needle drawn toward a lodestone.

Still garbed in their painted armor, the soldiers now set up camp in a pattern of tight concentric circles which, from the sky, must have looked like a giant four-colored flower. In the very middle of the camp was a giant pavilion of sheepskin. Atop its six-sided roof flapped the tassled flag of the Lady of Mongaul. Pages carrying orders moved in and out of the pavilion, while busy attendants to the lady disappeared inside carrying various containers and soft blankets they had taken from the train of pack horses. Inside the pavilion, the captains of the army, summoned to receive their latest orders, stood waiting for their lady-general to speak.

This was no concern of the knights and foot soldiers outside, whose greatest desire was rest; they stole time as they could to curl up and try to nap in the dry, thin twilight of the Nospherus dawn. The troops were filled with unease, for everywhere they looked, they saw twisted howling faces in the sand, phantasms from the legends and stories they had heard about the horrid denizens of the desert. The men on patrol found themselves constantly looking over their shoulders, tormented by visions of Sem warriors in warpaint bearing stone axes, attackers who would rush like demons across the shifting sands and sneak up during a moment's inattention. The sentries slipped and stumbled in the sand, which was a dust so fine that one could grab a handful one moment and be left holding nothing the next.

More than half of the Mongauli soldiers were originally members of the Marches patrol and came from the keeps of Alvon, Tauride, and Talos. They at least were somewhat accustomed to seeing the ashen wasteland in which they now stood, though they had mostly gazed on it only from the other side of the Kes. All but a few of them had seen a Sem warrior before, and they knew of the strange and terrible creatures that made Nospherus their home. But none amongst them had ever been further into the wastes than a day's journey on horseback.

There were stories that had spread through the Marches of people who were drawn by some inexplicable need to cross the wildlands. These stories, or legends, were mostly of the sort in which a youth would leave his home in Torus and cross the Kes, never to be seen again. Perhaps a band of merchants would go in search of the abandoned city of Kanan, driven by a mad obsession to find its rumored stores of gold. Tales of adventurers, and outlaws, and dreamers, they all had one thing in common: failure in the end and despair. If one believed all the tales, there were quite a few humans who had ventured deeper into the wildlands than the soldiers were now, but not once in the long history of Nospherus had any of these returned.

Of course, even those soldiers who had come from Torus, which was at a safe remove from the Marches, knew the stories, too. Wary of punishment, they did not speak their fears aloud, but in the gloom of the night, the Mongauli officers and men put mouth to ear and ear to mouth and cursed their ill fortune that they had to partake in an expedition so reckless. They shook their heads at the audacity of the whole thing and the direction of their own fate. Some of the more superstitious among them wondered in hushed voices about the evil spirits that must have possessed their commanders to make them think of such a foolhardy plan.

The unease of the troops also hung on the minds of the captains now gathered in the general's pavilion.

"Please allow me to ask a question." The one who spoke was Count Marus, lord of Tauride Castle and leader of two thousand blue knights.

"What is it, Marus?" Lady Amnelis, General of the Right and the daughter of Archduke Vlad, fixed the captain of the blue with a sharp stare. She was in a foul temper and not inclined to be indulgent. This had been the case since the march began, though it was unlikely that Amnelis herself knew the true source of her unease. In fact, her foul mood went back to her encounter with the strange, leopard-headed warrior and the twins of Parros. She had been roundly insulted by them, by prisoners in her own pavilion! And then, they had escaped.

Now she and her captains were gathered around a planning table upon which she had laid out a large map of Nospherus, inked in black on a giant sheet of sheepskin parchment. In several places there were red and blue markings.

Standing across from the lady-general, the commanders of the invading army looked down at the map intently, none wanting to draw a cold look from the archduke's daughter. On the far right stood Count Marus, the only one meeting her gaze. Next to him was Irrim, second-in-command at Talos Keep and leader of two thousand black knights. On Irrim's other side stood Captain Tangard, who had command of the footmen from Talos. Next to him were Leegan, son of Count Ricard the keep-lord of Alvon, and young Astrias. The "Red Lion of Gohra" was burning with shame and eager to vindicate himself after returning alive from battle with the Sem with only a handful of his troop. Finally, Count Vlon and Baron Lindrot, leaders of the white directly under Amnelis, stood off to the side.

The lady-general held a haughty pose, her blond hair flowing like a river of gold over her shoulders. Gajus Runecaster lurked in the shadows behind her. Next to him was the white knight Feldrik. And there was one more sitting silently in the gloom of the pavilion. None of the captains knew who he was or where he had come from.

The stranger had been with them from the beginning of the march, riding the whole way concealed in a palanquin with long curtains of cloth hanging down on all four sides, like those used to carry women in the eastern lands. None of the Mongauli soldiers had known who or what was inside. The cloth was too thick to peek through, and they had whispered quietly amongst themselves and taken bets on whose guess would prove to be correct. But none could say with any certainty who the passenger might be.

Even the captains were full of curiosity, for they had been told nothing about the mysterious guest who now sat in the gloom. He had been one of the last to cross the Kes, and had been surrounded by white knights afterwards, riding abreast of Amnelis's horse. But even though they had stopped for short breaks many times, the flaps of the palanquin had never opened.

When the captains first entered the pavilion and saw him standing with Amnelis, they had looked up expectantly, thinking that the guessing was finally over. But they had been disappointed. Since exiting the palanquin, the mysterious figure had kept a large hood over his face. A thick robe and cloak wrapped around his body so tightly that not a bit of him showed.

The guest's outfit was similar to the garb that Caster Gajus wore. The Mongauli captains were confronted by a peculiar tableau: two black gods of death standing to either side of the golden goddess of the dawn that was Amnelis. Still, even Gajus showed his weathered ugly face from under his hood, and he held his paper-thin hands out under his cloak and crossed them meditatively atop his chest, while the other one, whom they now thought must be a spellcaster, held his hands deep within the folds of his robes and never raised his head, so that his eyes met no one's from underneath that bulky hood. This piqued the curiosity of the captains even further, and they began to wonder if there was even a human being under those deep black robes.

Count Marus shot his eyes in the direction of the stranger, then hurriedly turned them away with a flustered look, as though he had seen something he should not have.

"Please let me ask a question," he said, repeating his request to the lady-general. "We lords of Mongaul received due orders to join under your command, and so we have, bringing much of the Marches patrol with us on this expedition into Nospherus. But still we have not been told what the Golden Scorpion Palace has in mind for us, what objective has brought this sizeable force here to this wasteland. We do not even know how long this expedition will last!" The count's voice rose at the end, perhaps a bit too much.

"I will tell you all in due time," Amnelis answered curtly. "As I believe I have said to you already, Count Marus." Her voice was icy and flat.

"But when will that be, my lady?" the count pressed, undaunted by the General of the Right, who was easily young enough to be his own daughter. "At least, tell our purpose for being here, and give us a general idea of how long we must be absent from our posts in the Mongauli Marches."

Amnelis did not answer. A slight look of hesitation passed over her fair, noble features.

"General," he persisted. Of the captains with whom he stood, he was the oldest, and he held the highest rank among the Gohran nobility, that of count. "The soldiers are uneasy, and when we who lead them are ourselves uncertain, they will be driven to further worry."

"Are the soldiers of Mongaul not the hands and feet of Mongaul, content to do what the mind tells them, as they have sworn to do?" asked Amnelis. "And must I clear where I go and what I do with all of my soldiers before I act?"

"General…" the white knight Feldrik spoke from behind her, trying to calm the supreme head of his order.

Count Marus took a deep breath. "That is not the case," he said, also trying to calm her. "Still, in order to ease the soldiers' fears, we must give them at least a modicum of information. They are, to say the least, curious about our destination. It troubles them to be this deep into the wildlands of Nospherus, following paths no army has tread in a land from which no one has returned."

"At first we believed," broke in Leegan, trying to be helpful, "that our expedition was a campaign to punish the Sem who so craftily attacked Stafolos Keep. Clearly, we must uphold the authority of Mongaul." The face of the young viscount, the son of Count Ricard, looked much like his father's. "But now we worry if it is wise to go so deep into the wildlands like this looking for the Sem villages."

"There is no need for worry." Amnelis waved a slender hand, irritated. Yet she knew it was required of her to explain the purpose of the great invasion ere long. Indeed, she had spared the time for this meeting of the captains for just that reason. This was the hour, when all was quiet as dawn broke over the camp. "Very well," she said. For a while she was silent as she considered how best to begin her explanation. She raised her face and looked at her captains.

Her cold, green eyes passed over Count Marus, Captain Irrim, Captain Tangard, and Viscount Leegan in turn, and then rested on Astrias, who stood at the end of the row. This young noble of Torus was only twenty, yet he had already made a name for himself throughout the archduchies. Since entering the pavilion, the captain had fixed his eyes on the lady-general's young, porcelain face in wordless reverence of her beauty.

But when his eyes met her cold, distrustful glare, the red knight's fine-featured face turned a bright shade of crimson. He was taken off guard, and abashed, lowered his face. Amnelis, sensing something, stared at him piercingly for a moment, but then turned away from him toward the white knights Vlon and Lindrot.

"Do you have proof that the soldiers' morale is wavering, Marus?" she asked, without looking at the count.

The commander of the blue raised his hands. "Right now, no. But if we do not soon tell them where we are going and what your Ladyship's plans are, rumors and speculation will spread through the troops like wildfire, and by the day's end I am afraid we will have a serious problem."

"I see," said Amnelis, deep in thought. "I had expected more from our Marches patrol. Only one day has passed since we cut into Nospherus. And the Sem have not attacked us once."

"While I said that we have no solid proof of our troops' unease," Marus added, "I did hear a rumor that came up through the ranks just before we were summoned here to this meeting. Apparently, some of the soldiers think that this expedition has not come to punish the Sem, and as evidence, they point—"

"What now?" cut in Amnelis, her face stern.

"As evidence," Marus continued, "they point to the fact that the scouts are not being sent out in all directions to find the Sem nest, as one might expect. Instead, your orders have been for them to scout straight east, in one direction only, as though we had a predetermined destination."

"Soldiers fascinate me. They see when they appear not to be looking, and they claim to know nothing but still must know everything," Amnelis remarked, a wry smile crossing her well-formed lips. "Their eyes are rather sharp, and accurate. Count Marus, your troops are correct," she admitted.

A stir went through the line of captains—but only a mild one, for they had already been expecting something like this.

"Of course," Amnelis continued, "the extermination of the Sem is one of the primary goals of this expedition, as you are all aware. But it is true that our final destination lies not in the villages of the Sem. It is…" Amnelis stuck out her index finger with a graceful swing of her hand, and then with sudden violence she thrust it down on a spot on the map laid out before her. "Here!"

The captains swallowed and looked at the spot where her unwavering finger stood.

Because Nospherus was largely unexplored by the people of the Middle Country, there were no detailed maps of it. The Mongauli map was really more white parchment than map, blank for the most part, except for where small mountains had been drawn in, along with a few place names, most of these located in the surrounding regions and not in Nospherus itself.

A wavering black line traced the edge of Nospherus closest to Amnelis. This was the River Kes, surrounded on the map by small red and blue markings showing the locations of troops of knights. But where Amnelis now pointed was far beyond the Kes, about in the middle of the parchment, a spot in a sea of white where hardly anything had been drawn.

"My lady, that..." Marus began with nervous diffidence, but Amnelis lightly motioned for him to be silent, and straightening up she looked over the captains once again.

"The Sem call this area *Gur Nuu*, the Valley of Death. It is this valley towards which we ride." There was not a trace of hesitation in her voice. The Mongauli captains glanced at each other for signs that any of them had heard of this place, but all faces were blank.

"We have already made it this far," Amnelis continued, tapping at a red *x* mark on the map much closer to her than the location of Gur Nuu. "I believe we have now come far enough into Nospherus that there is no fear of our secrets reaching the ears of other countries. I will tell you now what the ultimate purpose of our expedition is: we will find this Valley of Death, flatten the Sem tribes in the area, build a new fortress near the valley and claim it as our own. In fact, you have my permission to tell the troops as much." Her voice was low and relaxed, yet her words seemed to fill the pavilion.

The effect on the captains was that of a flaming catapult projectile plunging into their midst. They all began shouting at once, at her and at each other, as though they had all suffered amnesia and entirely forgotten the strict rules of military conduct .

"Amnelis, th-that..." Count Marus, his voice choking, made to protest. "For what possible reason—"

"Didn't I tell you not to call me by my name? I am no longer the child who once sat on your lap and called you uncle."

"My apologies, General." The old count lowered his head quickly, red faced.

Their brief exchange was lost in the excitement within the pavilion.

"Silence! I must have silence!" Amnelis shouted, slamming her fists down on the table. Abruptly, the room fell quiet. Eyes full of surprise and uncertainty looked across at their slender general.

"My lady, grant me permission to ask another question," Count Marus requested, his voice sounding stronger than before in the sudden silence. "We know of Mongaul's position since the fall of Parros, and we all appreciate our delicate political situation...but *because* of that very situation, I don't see..."

"Why fifteen thousand valuable troops have been sent into this wasteland?"

"...Yes," Marus confirmed, his shoulders slumping.

Should he anger the lady-general now, no amount of noble status—not even the fact that he had been her steward when she was little—would save him from her wrath.

"There is good reason, my captains," Amnelis said calmly. The anger that had crackled in her voice just moments before was gone, and now to everyone's surprise she wore a smile and almost seemed pleased; there was a hint of color in her lips. "Let me introduce that reason to you. Come forth, Cal Moru, and take off your hood." The lady-general turned and beckoned to the mysterious one who waited behind her.

The man stood and moved close to her, and swept his hood back over his head.

The cry that rose up from the captains was one of genuine astonishment and palpable fear. The sight was bizarre enough to wither even the iron self-control of seasoned warriors.

"I bring before you Cal Moru." Amnelis's voice was sharp with pride, echoing in the quiet of the pavilion. "He is a spell-caster—and the first person since the world was born to cross through the wildlands of Nospherus...and return!"

— 2 —

For a while it was all the Mongauli captains could do to simply remain standing as they looked at the man Amnelis called
"Cal Moru." The face that weighty hood had lifted to reveal was
freakish and cruel—a horrid thing that no man would care to
look upon twice. It was not merely ugly; it was the face of a living
corpse, only, more horrible still—a skull plastered with a thin,
baked leaf of skin. Only a few teeth remained clinging to the
thin gums that jutted from the crack that must have been the
mouth. Yet in that visage of death, the eyes, set in sunken sock-
ets, shone with a terrible brightness.

Is it human? The thought came unbidden to the captains'
minds once those minds began to work again. *How can this be?*
But this man was no victim of the black death, that they could
see. The skin of one afflicted with that disease drooped in folds
like wet, melted wax, but this one's skin was dry, as though all
the blood had been drained centuries past.

It was impossible to tell what that bizarre face might have looked like before the unknown, terrible events that had made it look as it now did. And his eyes! They shone in the dim light of the pavilion, returning the stares of the captains as though the mind behind them were not the least bit aware of the terror that gaze would cause in any sane man. After a while, Amnelis decided the captains had seen enough, and on her signal, the man slowly replaced his deep hood and concealed the dreadful sight.

The spell on the captains was released, and they woke from their stupor and breathed sighs of relief. There was something in Cal Moru's face that had caused them to tremble and fear for their very souls, perhaps because to look on that face was to wonder what possible chain of events could have changed a human—if, indeed, he had ever been human—into something so alien.

"Cal Moru comes from the land of Kitai, in the east." Whether she had become used to the sight of his face, or whether there was something unshakeable in her nature, the eighteen-year-old daughter of the archduke spoke without a trace of the horror that still lurked in the captains' minds. "As a young spellcaster, eager to master the high secrets of his art, Cal Moru was consumed by a desire to meet the legendary magus, Agrippa, and become his disciple. Is that not so?"

The creature gently nodded his head, a motion barely visible within the heavy folds of the hood.

"Agrippa?!" stammered Viscount Leegan. "But Agrippa is said to have been born many thousands, no, tens of thousands of years ago. Yes, they do say he lives an eternity, but there are none who really believe that!"

"But, Leegan," said Amnelis, raising her hands like an oracle about to deliver a revelation from the gods, "Cal Moru did. And that is not all—he believed he had proof. That proof is something that only spellcasters might comprehend, and so I will not speak of it now. Suffice it to say that Cal Moru had heard that the legendary Agrippa was alive somewhere in this world, working his secret alchemy, and so he left his homeland of Kitai to find him.

"He thought the lost sage would most likely be found in the Kanan Mountains, and so he explored the peaks and looked for signs of the ancient empire of Kanan. But there he found nothing, and so he continued on to the barren wastelands of Nospherus."

The captains listened, holding their breath. The story she was telling was surely nothing more than a fairy tale! Yet the captains did not have the luxury of disbelieving, for they could see Cal Moru right there before them.

"Of course," said Amnelis, "for a man to cross the wastes of

Nospherus and emerge alive is not something many of us think possible, not even in a dream. However, Cal Moru is no ordinary man. He is a spellcaster. He knows many secret arts, and at the time he was a strong, young man—far stronger than any of us here." At this the captains cast dubious glances in the direction of the living corpse, thankfully still hidden in his robes.

"And Cal Moru was blessed by good luck," Amnelis went on, once again drawing looks from the captains. "Unafraid of the wastes, he walked over great and terrible distances, and walked, and walked."

"Allow me to tell the story that follows, if I may," a voice sounded suddenly from beneath the hood, and the captains froze. It did not seem possible that this living corpse could speak, yet speak it did. Cal Moru's voice, issuing from the lipless crack of his mouth, was low and ragged. It was like a wind blowing through long-abandoned ruins.

"I walked," came the dry and evil-sounding voice. "Even were I a caster of considerable skill in the arts, to cross Nospherus would be no easy task. In the forbidden black magicks, there is an ancient art that allows one to warp the very fabric of space and time to one's liking, but I had not that art. I had to walk on my own weary feet and thus seek out the hiding place of the great Agrippa.

"So I walked. I battled with the sand leeches, and I scraped off the vampiric sand moss where it grew on my boots and the hem of my robes, and I hastily diverted my course when I happened upon the village of the Lagon barbarians. I walked for what seemed an eternity but was in fact several months, trekking through the endless rocks and sand in my search.

"I did not lack for food or drink, for even a humble spellcaster such as myself knows the arts of creating nourishment from nothing, and of floating in the air to sleep in safety. As I walked, I learned something about this land of Nospherus, something that sets this place apart. The people of my country call this a land forsaken by the gods, and what I saw made me agree, for all the plants and animals of this place have monstrous forms. Nothing is natural. It is as if the entire region had been brought here from another star, so alien is this land.

"Because spellcasters study the ways of plants and animals, I understood how unnatural these things that I saw were. This served to strengthen my certainty that, were the great Agrippa truly alive, such would be the place he would choose in which to conduct his experiments. As evidence that I drew close to him, I had noticed that the otherworldly air of Nospherus—the miasma of this place—had clouded the crystal sphere I had brought with me on my journey. Try as I might, I could not clear it.

"Then, when I woke up one morning, I found that my

sphere had gone jet black, and the moment I reached out my fingers to touch it, it fell to the ground and shattered. Then, to my further surprise, the pieces evaporated, leaving not one trace!"

No one in the pavilion uttered a word. Even Amnelis, who surely had heard this story many times before, was quiet. She listened intently, as though not wanting to miss a single detail.

"Rather than take the event as an ill omen," continued Cal Moru, his voice even and calm, "I felt that it was a sign that I was close to the great Agrippa for whom I searched. Agrippa had learned his arts from the ancient ones, the old gods—and thus his arts were anathema to Janos and his pantheon. My sphere had touched this ancient power, and that was why it broke, I reasoned. In truth, for several days I had been feeling an unusually strong presence, an otherworldly spirit in the air. As I progressed on my journey, the feeling only became stronger. With my spellcaster's senses, I felt as if I were walking into a waterfall of keening noise, shining light, and overpowering smell. This, I thought, this is the miasma of Agrippa, for none other than Agrippa—not even the demon-god Doal himself—could exude such a strong presence in all the four directions. It was something that had no connection with the pattern of life and magic in this world.

"Like a moth drawn to a flame, I continued walking on

towards the center of that miasma. And then, one morning..."

Cal Moru paused. Briefly he appeared to rest beneath his hood. A few tense moments passed in silence before, just as suddenly, he resumed his tale.

"One morning, I noticed a distinct change in the scenery around me. I had reached an otherworldly place, remarkable even here in the wastes of Nospherus, this land outside the domain of man which is, itself, called a place of death, and is populated by wildling barbarians and all manners of monstrosities. The place I had entered was verily a valley of death, a land made of bones that lay in a blanket of ghostly white—surely the design of some fickle demon. No, to call it a valley of death would cheapen it. It was not a place that could be described in the language we speak, or any other the human tongue is equipped to utter.

"The bones under my feet were a mottled white and gray, and very brittle. They crunched and crinkled when I walked upon them, sending up clouds of gray ash. I looked down at my feet—and then I realized: this land, this bone, was once as alive as I was. In the end, all of us are naught but bones, bones, and more bones. And among those bones lying there I saw something like the rib of a gigantic ancient beast, sticking straight up towards the sky as though it still begrudged the life that had been taken from it. And I could make out smaller bones, human-like, probably once belonging to the Sem.

"They were all so very brittle, so white, and—" Here Cal Moru gasped, remembering what it had been like to stand in that place, and the startled captains gasped in turn. "I realized that what I was standing on was a field of bone, and beyond it I could see a bone forest, a bone jungle, a bone island floating on a bone sea! And nowhere was there anything moving, anything alive. It was as though death had taken shape and appeared before me and I knew then the color of death. It is white and ashen gray.

"I remember that I stood there, speechless, my thoughts forming slowly as though I were in a dream. *How can this be?* I asked. *This is not the work of Agrippa!* Though Agrippa is a man of legend and believed in the ancient gods, still he is human! But this, this was not something that could be wrought by a man. No human being from any time or any land I knew of could even think of creating such a thing. It was not possible. Even I, a spellcaster of some standing who had participated in the secret rites of black magic and feared nothing, was stricken. The death I saw there was so terrible and so incomprehensible that it threatened to plunge me into an abject terror deep beyond all deepness in which I feared I would forget myself and lose my mind.

"For a while, my self-control and my power of reason

quailed to uselessness. When I came to my senses, I was on my knees, scooping up handfuls of the dry, brittle bone in my hands. I do not know what process those bones had endured, but all it took was the slightest touch—they would shatter and scatter in the wind. I could not say what kind of spell, what overwhelming magic had transformed this place into a hell on our earth. Suddenly a burning need to know filled me, and I found myself walking toward the center of the valley. It was easy enough to find my way, for all the bones as they lay on the ground were pointing in one direction and I knew this had to be toward the heart of the place.

"I did not know why, but my body felt incredibly heavy, as though it were filled with lead, and my throat became painfully parched. I could feel all the strength leaving my body. Yet I did not wonder at these things, for my mind had long since ceased all rational thought, and my soul was locked in a nightmare. I had no power to feel, no strength to suspect—all of that, was lost to me. I had forgotten who I was...

"I staggered on, crushing the bones beneath my feet, until I looked upon what I knew to be the center of the valley. There, to my surprise, was nothing of the kind I expected—no palace of Agrippa, no gaping hell-chasm out of which noxious vapors spewed. All that was there was a large rock. But this rock—it was an ugly, misshapen thing, pitted with pockmarks.

"*Why?* I thought, or thought I thought, deep in my paralyzed and terribly heavy brain. How could this rock—this entirely ordinary rock—turn the surrounding land, three tads in all directions, into a valley of death, a forest of bone? It was as though thousands of creatures had been drawn there, to a stone, and approaching it had perished, leaving their skeletons facing the center of the valley as evidence of their fatal endeavor. The bones to the north lay facing south, and those to the south lay facing north, in a great circle around that stone.

"*This is no ordinary rock*, I thought, *no ordinary thing! This rock hides some terrible, dark secret!* Then, foolishly—perhaps it was because of the paralysis that gripped my brain and made me forget all caution, all instinct—I stretched out my hand and touched a piece of that rock.

"I do not know if you can believe me, but when I laid my hand upon that rock, I felt a strange sensation in my fingers. I stood there dumbfounded and looked at my hand. Or rather, I should say, looked at where my hand had been. Before my eyes, the flesh on my fingers eroded and evaporated into thin air. In the blink of an eye, my hand crumbled down to bone, leaving no trace of living flesh beyond my wrist."

Cal Moru thrust his right hand out from underneath his cloak. The captains averted their eyes, for his hand, from the wrist to the tips of his fingers, was nothing but bones.

"Oddly enough," the scarred spellcaster continued, "I felt no pain. That is to say, it happened so fast I did not have time to feel pain. Stupefied by these events, I stared up into the sky. Bone ash danced higher and higher above me, and it was as though even the wheel of the sun was wrapped in a veil of pallid cinders. Then I saw something black rip through the white veil that obscured my vision. It was a lone desert crow. It flew through the miasmal air over that valley of death as though naught were amiss, until, suddenly, it began to dive, flapping its wings. Then it fell like a stone.

"The crow fell toward that circle at the base of the rock, no wider than a single pace, where there was no bone, as though all the skeletons had made a wordless pact not to approach any closer. There, the bare ground was made of iron sand the color of blood. Then, the very instant the crow fell, there was a whooshing sound, and the bird simply...evaporated, leaving no trace that anything ever living had been there—just as my right hand had lost all life.

"*The life-killing stone...the valley of the life-killing stone, Gur Nuu!* The words ran through my head. Then a thought formed, powerful, at the nethermost layer of my consciousness: I had to escape the place.

"There is something I should explain before I go on," croaked Cal Moru. "We spellcasters are not entirely human, you see. The trainings and processes we undergo to make our bodies suitable for channeling the elements of our trade change our very nature and structure. Our flesh becomes more spiritual, much deeper than ordinary flesh, and in response our spirit becomes more flesh-like and takes on physical form. In this way, we are able to change our shapes into those of other things, and our bodies become better attuned to the many and various energies of the universe.

"If this had not been the case, then I can only surmise that, had I been only foolish enough to come within a few hundred motad of that stone, its miasma would still have grasped my life and taken it from me, as it had done to the other beasts that had met their end in that valley. Even for one such as me, a spell-caster, standing there for a *twist* had taken its toll. My sanity was waning, and the strength had left my body. I felt that, if the wind blew up, I would crumble. I wanted to lie down, but I knew that doing that would seal my fate—the bitter lesson of my right hand had taught me that.

"I do not know how I lived to escape Gur Nuu, nor what strength of will and spirit carried me to its edge, for during that trek my mind reeled as though I were intoxicated. I remember nothing of my escape. When I came to my senses, I was lying in the middle of the familiar rock and sand of Nospherus. My soul had reached the limits of its endurance, and I had fallen. I say, I do not know how I escaped from that hell. Perhaps I did not survive, I thought back then, and I was no more than a wandering ghost; I had no way of confirming this one way or another. My thoughts were filled with pain, and I think I went mad. One thing I was sure of was that all my humanity had abandoned me. I was a shell, a cursed husk of a man.

"I walked on unsteady legs, and no matter how far I went, the barren scenery did not change. For a time I feared that, after my encounter with the stone, it had spread its miasma throughout the world, making every land into a soulless place, killing all life. There was nothing growing and I could sense nothing alive.

"I remember once that a kind Sem called to me. He called to me in that high-pitched voice of their kind, asking if I needed help. I was filled with joy that there was still life, and the world had not ended, and for the first time I felt a burning thirst in my throat. But when I lifted my head, revealing my face…the Sem ran away, leaving only a scream of terror.

"I suspiciously thrust out the skeletal remains of my hand into the glazed pot the Sem had dropped when he ran, and I praised the gods, for it was water. But when I looked at the surface of the water I completely forgot about my parched throat, and stared hard and unblinkingly at what I saw there. All the flesh that could be called flesh had burned and melted away from my face, and it had become as you saw it just now—a living skull—inhabited only by my swollen tongue, thrusting out painfully from between my jaws, and by my two eyes open in eternal terror, never to close again. And so I became a living corpse, returned from hell itself."

The captains of Mongaul were speechless.

"Cal Moru made his way to the Kes River," said Amnelis. "There, he was rescued by settlers." The general's voice, high and clear, blew like a breeze through the pavilion, sweeping away the chill that had frozen the men in place. "The settlers feared that Cal Moru carried a contagious disease, but when they heard his story, they quietly handed him over to the Marches patrol. Word of his adventure passed through them on to Torus, and that is why we are now here."

Amnelis related this with a finality that made it clear to the captains that she intended them to learn no more. She brusquely dismissed them with orders to begin the march again in two *twists'* time. None of the captains felt any need to ask questions. They were utterly astonished by the tale; without a word more, they exited from the lady-general's pavilion, glad to be outside.

Only the lady-general herself, Gajus Runecaster, the mysterious Cal Moru, and one other remained inside.

"What is it, Count Marus?" Amnelis asked, turning a cold

glare at the noble. Marus was quite old, but he was in no way decrepit. His face was stern and drawn, a warrior's face, and it was clouded with concern for the lady over whom he had watched ever since she was born.

"So, this is the reason why the Golden Scorpion Palace moves into Nospherus with the speed of spreading flame?" he asked in a low voice, moving around the table to stand next to the general.

"What are you trying to say, Uncle? You think the Palace acts unwisely?" Amnelis flared.

"If I may be so bold," said Count Marus, a flicker of deep unease in his eyes, "I have not felt at ease ever since the orphans of Parros escaped. As you know, we all have orders to find and capture them."

"We have not given up our search for the twins, nor our efforts to divine the secrets of the device that allowed them to escape the crystal city." Amnelis's beautiful face was twisted by a bitter look of frustration. She remembered the little girl Rinda, a princess without a country, and how she had stood before her in defiance, heedless that Amnelis was the general of a mighty army. "In any case we can assume they've holed up in some Sem village, or have met their end in these wastelands. Either is acceptable—what matters is that their secrets do not pass to another country. If we do capture the twins of Parros, we will drag those secrets out into the light, whatever means we must use to do so. None of that, however, eclipses the importance of what Cal Moru has found. Or do you disagree with the Golden Scorpion Palace?"

Amnelis paced as she continued, "Right now, both these secrets are firmly in our hands. No country but Mongaul has claim to them. And once we have grasped these mysteries—the mystery of the transportation device and the mystery of the rock that kills all it touches—Mongaul can conquer the other two archduchies, and even the whole of the Middle Country." She smiled, a cold smile that froze Count Marus's heart. "And why stop there?" the young general added, more to herself than to him. "Why not rule the world?"

"Amnelis, Amnelis!" said the count, entirely forgetting he had been forbidden the use of her name. "I...have a horrible feeling about this. Nothing good can come from possessing a weapon of that power! This is beyond the ken of humans! It is Doal's work, this thing that would curse anything it touches. It has to be."

"If you believe that, then you are a fool," Amnelis snorted. "A weapon is merely a weapon, nothing more. What matters is how you use it." She smiled at him without warmth. Then, in a tired voice, she declared that it was time for her to sleep in preparation for the next leg of the march.

That was Count Marus's signal to leave, and, bowing curtly, he stepped out of the pavilion. But his face held a look of great anxiety. "Weapons use people, too, sweet Amnelis," he said to the morning sun. "You are young...too young!"

The only answer from the pavilion was silence.

3

The general's pavilion was shrouded in sleep. Even the last orange torchlight spilling out through the cracks between its woven panels had been extinguished.

Around the camp, the knights who were not on watch curled up beside their bedded-down horses and rolled their bodies in their thick blankets until they looked like giant larvae on the sand trying to wrap themselves in sleep's elusive web. The blankets they used were actually the same ones which the knights placed beneath their saddles to ease the jarring ride across the desert—and which, when each stage of the journey was over, they employed for all manner of camp purposes, as bedding, cover, or even impromptu dining tables.

From afar, the Mongauli host looked like nothing so much as a giant mushroom that had suddenly sprung up in the middle of the dark, featureless Nospherus landscape. From that mushroom, sentries had gone out like tiny spores into the night. Bearing spears and wearing faintly gleaming helmets, their long cloaks fluttering behind them, blue, red, black and white silhouettes had stood in the dark.

Now the bluish purple of the predawn sky stretched above their heads. It was a startlingly gentle and beautiful hue for such a forsaken place, so far into the Marches. Yet few looked up to appreciate it. When a soldier did look up, it was to curse the lingering gloom. Most of them watched the horizon, praying for day to come soon and protect them from the threat of the Sem who they imagined were lurking in every shadow, and around every boulder.

One of the patrolmen stopped suddenly, and raised his spear. "Who goes there?" he demanded in a low voice. "Ah, I beg your pardon, lord captain," he stammered a moment later, quickly lowering his weapon as the young Astrias, a captain of the red, appeared from behind a rocky outcropping.

"Good work. Keep up your watch," said the dashing noble. It seemed he did not need rest, for he had been away from his horse and crude bedroll, pacing the perimeter of the camp, breathing in the clear air of the day's beginning.

Even in full armor, the captain cut a slender figure against the sky. He placed his hands at his waist and drew himself up to his full height to look out over the horizon. His handsome profile was smudged by a day's growth of beard that made him look somehow wiser.

"What a woman! And still only eighteen," whispered Astrias to the dawning sky. He had taken off his plumed helm, and there was a dreamlike expression on his face, almost as though...no, it was unmistakable, he was in love.

"Sorry, Captain? Do you have an order for me, sir?"

"Ah, no, it is nothing," Astrias replied, glancing over at where the attentive sentry stood. He could feel the color rising to his cheeks, and he thanked the lingering gloom that it could not be seen.

The sentry stared at the young captain, the Red Lion of Gohra, beloved of all the troops. Fearing that he would break his captain's reverie, he waited silently, eyes cast downward, only occasionally stealing glances up at Astrias. Finally, he made up his mind to speak, and managed a few nervous words.

"Lord Captain."

"What is it?"

"Might I... Might I ask you a question?"

"Go ahead."

"It is..." the soldier faltered. The captain knew what he wanted to ask but remained silent, looking out at the horizon, waiting for the soldier to finish. "It is concerning our destination." Now that he had begun to talk, the man relaxed, and feeling that he must ask now or never, he continued on. "There is a rumor among the troops, sir. They say that the Lady of Mongaul plans for us to conquer all of Nospherus, and that we may be here for a very long time. They fear that many of us will never make the journey home, not in this lifetime."

"And if it is so, do you not believe that as a soldier of Mongaul there can be no greater honor than to be part of such a grand undertaking? What is better than to have your bones buried to form a foundation for Mongauli glory in a foreign land?" Astrias's response was quick, and imperious—but then he relented and spoke more softly. "These rumors, are they widespread?" he asked, taking a step towards the soldier.

"Ah—"

"Do not fear me. Take off your helmet and speak clearly."

Fear raced through the sentry's mind that perhaps the captain wanted to remember the face of the one who had complained. But when he saw the friendly twinkle in the young captain's round, black eyes, he relaxed and removed his black helmet, holding it over his right breast in the formal salute of Mongaul. The soldier was hardly different in age from Astrias. But he was a footman, not assigned to any troop of knights; he was rather a conscript for the Marches patrol, probably the son of some borderland farmer. Mongaul had a levy which required all youths to join one of the patrols for a minimum of three years upon turning eighteen.

This soldier's sunburned face was soft and unrefined, a peasant's face. Astrias decided to be gentle to this one. "What our commander fears most is inaccurate information spreading unnecessary fears among the ranks. Tell me your name, soldier, and where you hail from."

"Marrel, sir. I am from the village of Luet in the county of Boa. I serve at Talos Keep."

"Well, Marrel, there will be an announcement to the troops soon, so I might as well tell you now. We are headed for a valley near the middle of Nospherus, a place called Gur Nuu."

"Sir!" said the astonished Marrel. "You mean we are not here to beat back the Sem tribes?"

"No. Or rather, that is not the most important objective," replied Astrias. "Punishing the Sem is still part of our mission. And I feel it likely that we will have at least one large battle with the Sem on our way to the Nospherus interior. But our final destination remains Gur Nuu. We will go to that valley and there build a fortress to claim the land as Mongauli territory. It will be our new stronghold in this region, to replace the fallen Stafolos."

"Gah! Sir, ay' cunna—" began the young soldier, the regional accent of Boa coming through in his shock. "That idea's crazier 'an Doal's frothin' horse, sir! I beg your pardon, but..." He looked up at Astrias's face, worried that he had offended the captain. Astrias's lips were curled in a sneer at the way he had said "frothing horse," making it sound like a single word: "frothinorse." Fearfully the man spoke on, trying to keep his accent in check. "Should that fortress be built, sir, we'd have to man it, wouldn't we? We'd be stuck in a fortress in the middle of nowhere, wasting our days fending off the Sem!"

"We are not even sure we will make it to Gur Nuu yet," snapped Astrias, losing his temper. "And who are you, a lowly foot soldier, to question the decisions of the Golden Scorpion Palace?" He glared at the quaking soldier briefly, then his face softened again. "Do not worry, Marrel. It is not we who will be stationed there. Why, we have not even brought an engineering corps with us. Should we find this valley, we would leave a small force there and hurry back to Alvon, from which a garrison force would then escort the castle-builders and supply caravans to Gur Nuu. Our duty, rather, is to drive out the Sem that stand in our way, and to find the location of this valley. Do not worry, you will be back in Alvon soon."

Marrel nodded, but he looked no less anxious. It was an understandable anxiety, for the worst fear shared by all the levied peasant-soldiers was that they would be sent to man a keep in some remote and hostile place where they would die during their service. Unlike the professional soldiers, the levied men had fields in need of tending waiting for them at home, and needy families as well. A posting to a place like Talos Keep, right on the River Kes, gave them cause to lament their ill fortune. But such an assignment was nothing compared to the prospect of being sent to man the ramparts of a castle deep in the heart of Nospherus and overlooking that terrifying wasteland.

But Astrias did not have time to concern himself with the despair of a mere foot soldier. The captain was still young, and filled with ambition. His commander, a woman two years his junior, was no other than the beautiful Amnelis. For the Red Lion, leaving the safety of Mongauli territory and heading deep into the wastelands of Nospherus was not a challenge that provoked despair, despite his uncertainty as to what lay ahead and his knowledge of many dangers that did threaten. His greatest concern was to find an opportunity to win the grand victory that would enhance his reputation throughout the three arch-duchies and bring recognition—admiration, even—from that young lady-general with the golden hair.

Even this barren wasteland, the domain of the Sem and all manner of horrendous creatures, appeared to Astrias's youthful heart a fertile field with precious stones hidden in its soil. He soon forgot the worried Marrel, and slipped back into his earlier reverie. At the center of his thoughts, shining with a bright incandescence, was the cold and beautiful face of the lady Amnelis. This morning was not the first time he had met her. Being of the noble class of Mongaul, he had had occasion to bask in her presence quite often for one who was not a member of the white knights.

At the great parties in the palace, she would always appear to tremendous fanfare and applause, wrapped in jeweled satin and silk almost too dazzling to look upon. Leading her sickly brother Mial by her left hand she would stand on the balcony and bow gracefully to the assembled lords and ladies, and then withdraw. In the palace, she was like a moon goddess appearing in her radiant beauty one moment, only to disappear behind clouds the next. She was both extraordinarily beautiful and impossibly distant.

But here, Astrias thought, *here in Nospherus, the radiant Aeris has come down to earth*. She was there, sleeping in that pavilion, which stood so close that he could have hit it with a stone. That stern, beautiful white face surely wandered in a maiden's sleep that none was permitted to disturb, her lips parted slightly, letting her sweet breath escape—beneath the blankets her bosom gently rising and falling. Asleep, she was just a fair girl of eighteen, nothing more. As soon as the order to march was given, however, she would place her helm on her head, hide her beauty behind an ornamented hood and cloak, and ride at the head of the troops atop her horse, a general once more.

Stronger than any man, braver than any warrior, more beautiful than any goddess...

Yet when Astrias had come to her on his knees with the report of his utter defeat and looked up at her, his eyes full of shame, the young lady-general of Mongaul had returned a glare that held not one shadow of charity, not a touch of softness.

How pitiful she must have thought me, to return routed by the Sem, escaping while my men died around me. How untrustworthy, how worthless a soldier I must be in her eyes! There was little chance she had noticed how he admired her beauty, or how deeply shocked and humiliated he was at his defeat. Yet Astrias, there in the harsh beauty of the Nospherus morning, could think of nothing but her.

May I protect her! What a burden for a maiden to bear—for she is destined to rule the entire Middle Country as the Empress of Mongaul one day... But no, she is more than a maiden. She is the avatar of Irana War-Goddess! Where, oh where in that slender form does she hide the courage and the strength to lead an army of fifteen thousand men on a march across the wilds of Nospherus? I must be her protector, even if it means my life! I would not have one strand of golden hair from that beautiful head come to harm at the hands of a filthy barbarian warrior. No matter what happens, I shall guard her, and return her safely back to Torus!

It did not occur to Astrias that if he truly managed to save the lady-general in such a manner, he might impress her enough to be put in the seat at her left, one day to succeed the archduke himself. Too young and too pure a warrior to consider such a scheme, it was with honor and innocence that Astrias turned wistful eyes to the lady-general's pavilion.

Neither did his thoughts linger on Cal Moru, the fearful and strange spellcaster who had come through the Valley of Death and now shared her pavilion; nor did he dwell on the grand and fearsome plans that Cal Moru's information had inspired the Golden Scorpion Palace to devise, and what that meant for the brave Mongauli warriors camped around him. All Astrias could see was Amnelis, and himself protecting her wherever she might lead them, fighting alongside her in battle, guarding her with his sworn blade.

"Eh?" Astrias lifted his eyes. "Someone plays the rigolo."

The rigolo was the most popular wind instrument in Mongaul, a simple flute made of a length of bamboo.

"Yes, Captain Astrias," answered Marrel of Luet. But Astrias had spoken to himself, entirely having forgotten in his daydreaming that he was not alone.

Some knight with a touch of romance in his heart had carried the instrument with him from Mongaul, thinking to calm the camp and relieve the tedium of the watch from time to time. The simple tune floated through the camp of fifteen thousand unquiet souls, ringing in the deep quiet of the Nospherus dawn.

Astrias's first impulse was to find the player and say something to him about the proper behavior of a soldier camped in enemy territory. He thought better of it, and stood silently listening to that melody from home. For Astrias, however, it was still too early to think of returning. He was too young to be yearning for peace, and the three years he had spent on the Marches in Alvon were fresher in his mind, and more exciting, than his dimming memories of life back in Torus.

Instead, he thought of Amnelis.

"The day is dawning," he said at last, pulling himself out of his reverie and looking around at the brightening horizon.

Over the course of the journey into Nospherus, little had changed in the seemingly endless plain of rock and lichen on either side of the marching army. The dry landscape was dotted with an occasional desiccated bush but otherwise stretched flat and featureless far in all directions. Still, the gray land had a strange, severe kind of beauty to it that touched the hearts of the men who were awake at that moment. It was a kind of beauty that went well with the humble melody of the rigolo.

Hmm?

Astrias wrinkled his brow. For a moment he thought he had seen something moving out in the distance. He watched carefully for a while, but nothing else moved and so he decided that he had been tricked by the morning light. All he could see was gently sloping rock and sand, as lifeless as ever.

"Say—" began Astrias, thinking to ask Marrel whether he had seen anything. He broke off when he saw that tears were streaming down the conscript's face. The song the rigolo played was a lullaby from the region of Boa.

Boa lay far from the Marches. It was a warm lowland, a basin with some of the most fertile farmland in all of Mongaul, warm enough to grow fruits in great quantities. How hard it must be on a youth from a verdant land such as that, the captain thought, to spend years in the Marches at Talos Keep, then to cross the black Kes into this wasteland. Feeling he should try to comfort him, but not knowing how, Astrias turned and walked away.

Hmm...

The sound of the rigolo had stopped mid-tune, as though cut off by some invisible hand. The wind, too, had died. The air was dead still, and despite the fifteen thousand troops there, the loneliness of the place became almost unbearable, pressing on the captain's ears with its horrible silence.

Astrias, seeing Marrel peering about, suddenly felt unsure of what to do. He noticed that the sun had risen completely, but this only made him feel horribly exposed as he stood there on the edge of camp.

Marrel didn't seem to have noticed anything out of the ordinary. He turned to look for the rigolo player, perhaps to

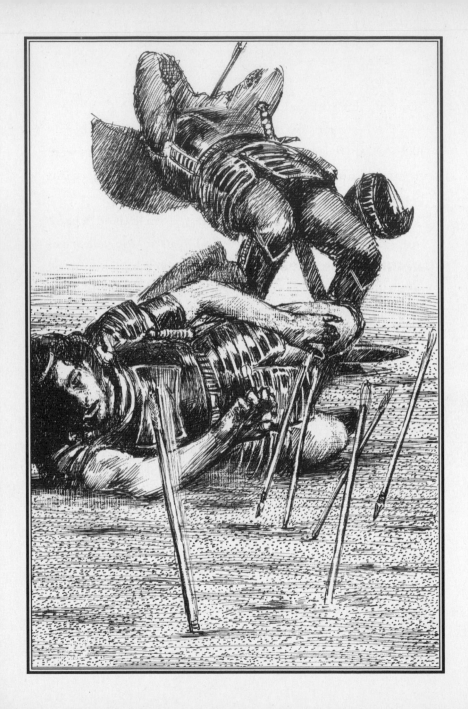

urge him to keep playing. His face was innocent as a child's. Astrias had a sudden, inexplicable urge to call out to him, to tell him to put on his helmet, but before he could act on it he heard the sharp whistling noise of something cutting through the air.

From Marrel's throat came a sound like the whistle of a flute. Astrias started. One minute the youth was standing, looking around for the rigolo player, and the next moment he was spinning his arms wildly, staggering in a circle. Then he fell headlong on the ash-gray Nospherus sand.

It all happened so fast that Astrias's mind could not comprehend what he saw. He stood for an instant staring stupidly at Marrel, who was falling with his eyes wide open, a short black feathered arrow in his neck.

Then the captain threw himself on the ground, narrowly dodging the next arrow that came flying, it seemed, out of nowhere. Where he had been standing just moments before, black feathers bristled on the ground like quills on the back of a hedgehog.

Rolling on one side, he drew his sword. There was no time to put on his helmet. He knew all too well the deadly poison that coated those arrows. Swinging his sword in a waterwheel pattern with the blinding speed of desperation, he knocked aside a storm of arrows, which clattered lightly off his blade.

Even as he did so, he ran, doubled over, back toward the center of the camp.

Then he froze. Around him the ashen sand was bubbling and rising!

No. It was not the ground that was moving, it was a troop of small hairy wildlings, looking ever so much like crazed monkeys. Garbed in tunics coated in birdlime and rubbed with sand, the Sem had spread a net of camouflage on the sandy ground and used it to approach within arrow range. Now they were throwing off the net.

The land split open before Astrias's eyes and its furry guts spilled upward. In an instant, the white and gray desert under that clear blue sky was filled with faces painted red and blue, vicious bared teeth, brown and black mottled fur, and the foul smell of a force of screaming wildlings.

"Aiii! Iiiya iiiya iiiya!"

Astrias stared in dismay, but he recovered quickly from the shock. Again he began to run, shouting, "The Sem! The Sem are attacking! To arms! To arms!" He was in the midst of a sea of furred warriors.

Above the screeching of the wildlings he heard the bronze gong calling the camp to battle and the battle cries of the Mongauli soldiers. The camp was answering the Sem challenge.

A furious battle was underway all around him.

He shouted wildly, for he now realized that the Sem had not attacked from one direction only, but from all sides. They were surrounded.

—— 4 ——

Of course, not enough Sem had come spilling out of the ground to actually surround the entire Mongauli army. Yet, to the surprised eyes of Astrias and the sleepy eyes of the march-weary troops, the wildlings seemed like a multitude, a swarm of twenty thousand or more boiling out of the ground on all sides. The men scrambled for their weapons, their hearts filled with fear.

Had any of the Mongauli soldiers had the presence of mind to look around with clear eyes, he would have realized that the human forces were superior in both numbers and equipment. Moreover, it was now fully light, and there were no rocks or bushes behind which to hide, a less than ideal situation for their attackers. But it was precisely because all these factors weighed so heavily in favor of the Mongauli that they had not expected this stealthy assault.

In keeping with their knowledge of the Sem's simple tactics, the Mongauli commanders had expected a different sort of attack, and preparations had been made accordingly. What the men feared most was a night assault in an open camp; that was why they had risked the dangers of a night march in Nospherus and only allowed the troops to rest once the sky began to brighten around them. Even a night passage through the wastes had seemed less perilous than a Sem night attack, in which the wildlings might have crept up to the commanders' very tents unobserved.

But now the day had dawned, and the sentries were watching in all directions. The Mongauli were superior in numbers, weapons, and sheer physical size compared to their enemies. The last thing the human army had expected was a daring assault in broad daylight. This overconfidence was the only chink in their armor, and through it the Sem had struck.

As part of their strategy, the Sem had made an effort to give the impression that they were coming from many different directions. All the wildling warriors had adorned themselves with bright warpaints and feathers to make themselves look larger and more numerous than they actually were. There was also a group of Sem who had slipped into a hidden hollow not far from camp, from which they beat on drums and blew warpipes, and screamed shrill war cries as they set fire to bundles of smokegrass they had brought with them, sending thick yellow smoke rolling through the camp.

In moments, the smoke drew a noxious yellow veil across the sun, plunging the camp into an eerie twilight. The Mongauli warriors coughed and choked on the fumes as they ran about in confusion, grasping at their swords, slamming into each other by accident, and sending up cries of fear.

Many of the soldiers who had been sleeping when the attack began were tangled in their bedding, falling and tripping others who ran past them. A band of Sem warriors added to the confusion by rushing to where the horses were tethered and using their pointed stone axes to cut the horses' flanks and sides, sending them whinnying and biting madly through the middle of the camp or bolting in fear in every direction. The thick yellow smoke, the galloping, whinnying horses, the beating drums, the screams of the soldiers, and the shouting of the captains giving orders all added to the chaos.

"Quiet! Quiet!"

"The Sem are attacking!"

"Grab your swords! Where are those bowmen? And the horses! Somebody grab the horses!"

Above it all the war cries of the Sem rang out. Madness reigned like a demon god.

The Sem invaders had bows, but they were already inside the camp. For the Mongauli crossbowmen to meet them with their hails of stone would have placed their comrades in a crossfire. Yet, having heard a captain's wild shouts for them, the soldiers faithfully followed their orders, sending lethal shots streaking through the clouds of yellow smoke at their tiny furry targets. Some shots flew true, but the vast majority went wide, denting Mongauli armor or punishing the flanks of horses. Soon a great number of the cavalry's steeds were racing uncontrolled among the milling soldiers or, their legs wounded, rolling and flailing among the tents. The Mongauli camp was sent spinning further out of control.

"Hold your shot! Put down your bows!" shouted Astrias, his voice already hoarse from yelling. "Meet them with swords!" The young captain ran through the haze, which had grown so thick that it had become difficult to tell friend from foe. His ears were full of the screams and clangor of battle and he struck out for all he was worth, cutting anything small and brown that got in his way. Already, his red armor was painted redder still with Sem blood. "Keep your wits about you! Throw down your bows, throw them down! Don't spread out, keep to one place and fight in clusters! Somebody calm those horses!" As he shouted, he ran toward the general's pavilion, one thought filling his mind. He must protect Amnelis!

Cutting down Sem left and right, he searched for the pavilion. The enemy had closed in on the camp, no doubt to prevent the Mongauli from using their powerful crossbows. But the maneuver also prevented the Sem from using their deadly poison arrows effectively. Instead, they wielded the stone axes that they carried at their waists; screaming in their high-pitched voices, they leapt through the air, splitting Mongauli soldiers' heads or swinging at their vulnerable knees.

The Sem attacked with great speed, but Astrias knew them to be reckless in battle, and he felt himself in little danger. As long as he was wary that no Sem circled around him to attack from behind, and as long as he kept his beloved sword away from the stone axes' shattering blows, he had little to fear. The small size of the Sem made it a simple matter for him to ward off their attacks.

When one Sem, his furry face painted an unsettling hue of scarlet, came leaping high with a howl and swung his wickedly sharp stone axe at Astrias's head, the captain nimbly stepped aside and brought down his blade with a chopping cut that split the Sem clean in two. Astrias jumped back neatly to avoid the spray of blood and brains. Dodging a puff of smoke, he turned back to look at the pavilion, then wiped his eyes and blinked.

The pavilion seemed unnaturally quiet. It was as if the lady-general were still sleeping inside, entirely unaware of the chaos raging all around, so calm did the great tent seem. Yet it was the brain of the Mongauli army, and the army was beginning to think once more.

The soldiers around the perimeter of the camp bore the brunt of the attack. Footmen, bowmen, and knights alike were caught unawares. None had the time to organize or to catch and control the bolting horses before the Sem were among them and everything was a chaotic mess of swords, cries, and battle. However, the interior of the camp had had time to listen to their captains' orders, and lines of defense had been formed swiftly with the lady-general's pavilion at their center.

Here at the heart of the camp, the Mongauli commanders had taken time to survey the situation and plan a course of action.

"Stay calm! Lower your faceplates!"

"We outnumber them! Watch their movements!"

"For Mongaul!"

The orders flew down the ranks, and finally, the knights began to act like the trained elites they were. They could see now that the only serious fighting with the enemy was confined to a shallow ring around the camp perimeter. Only a few groups of Sem had infiltrated the camp itself.

"They are few! The drums and smoke are a ruse!"

Messengers ran back and forth, carrying orders from the command center down to every squad captain. If one had looked down upon the wastes from high above, they would have seen the giant four-colored flower slowly bloom as the ranks formed and began to move in an organized fashion against their attackers.

"Leegan Corps, forward!"

"Irrim Corps, to the rear!"

"Tangard Corps, guard the left flank!"

"All white knights, surround the general's flag!"

Ensigns brought commands to the divisions whose color flag they bore, and as the orders were executed, the petals of the flower opened—the blue, black, and red all moving out in formation while the white gathered toward the center, a brilliant pistil in the center of a blossom that unfurled its furious petals in the wasteland.

The Sem scurried about like insects buzzing around that giant flower. But the knights had soon gotten most of the horses under control, and now the wildlings faced mounted opposition. Furthermore, the yellow smoke that had concealed their numbers at the opening of the battle was now mostly gone, blown away by the morning breeze. They had lost most of the advantage gained by their sneak attack, and now the tables were clearly turned against them.

"Irrim Corps, advance beyond the footmen!"

"Marus Corps, send your First Troop out into the desert! Find the wildlings making that smoke, and deal with them!"

"Feldrik, Lindrot, and Vlon, form ranks by the tent and await your orders."

The messengers moved through the troops efficiently, a spider web of guidance. All could see that the battle had turned. The Sem were divided by thrusts from the knights in formation, and they were being cut down one by one. Without the advantage of surprise, the small, poorly armed wildlings were no match for the elite riders of Mongaul.

By now, the soldiers were taking turns on the front lines, fresh men relieving their wearied comrades. Astrias, who had been surrounded by the fighting since the very beginning, now lowered his sword and traded places with another. Wiping the dripping blood off his blade, he strode back toward his own men. Since they had been positioned toward the middle of the camp, they were largely unharmed by the sneak attack.

"Lord Captain! Are you injured?" Astrias's lieutenant, Pollak, came running from among the ranks of red knights. "You look—you look like you've killed your share of monkeys, sir," said Pollak, his face easing into a grin.

"You expected different?" asked Astrias, returning his smile. "Monkey see..." he brandished his bloodied sword, "monkey die." He handed off his blade to a page and approached Pollak. "As you can see, I've not a scratch. Any wounded or dead among our corps?"

"Not a one," Pollak reported. "The men are disappointed that none of the enemy made it in this far. Ah, there was one injury, actually."

"Who?"

"Rilo, sir. He sprained his left arm trying to mount his horse. Got out the wrong side of his bed this morning."

"The fool!" exclaimed Astrias, laughing aloud.

"We were most worried about you, sir," Pollak admitted. He had been Astrias's right hand since they left Torus, and none knew the young captain better. "We called the rolls, and you were the only one missing."

"Can't a man take a morning stroll when he pleases anymore?" asked Astrias, sticking out his unshaven face in mock anger. The knights of the red around him laughed.

"Not if it means leaving your men and hoarding all the battle to yourself!" Pollak countered, smiling.

"There was no battle today, we were just playing with some monkeys. Pity about that Marrel..." he added with a frown, recalling the ruddy-cheeked footman of the Marches patrol who had listened to the tune of the rigolo with tears in his eyes.

"You should take a lesson from this," Pollak jested. "Next time you feel moved to take a stroll, bring a bodyguard."

Astrias was about to counter with a jibe of his own when a messenger with a white tassel hanging off his shoulder rode up and hailed him.

"Orders from the general. All captains are to give a report at once on the numbers of wounded, dead, and horses lost."

"Understood," responded Pollak on his captain's behalf, bowing to the messenger. "Lord Captain, it appears the first skirmish is over."

"Right. We have one wounded, then, and—what of our horses?"

"Margot's horse hurt its leg, but it is nothing serious. Nothing else."

"And the Sem, they have retreated?" Astrias asked. He stepped onto a boulder to peer toward the front, then nodded, satisfied. "Hmm, it seems so. I am afraid we did not kill all of them, though."

Throughout the camp the fighting had ceased. The Sem had pulled back with the same surprising speed with which they had attacked. Around the camp's perimeter the ground was strewn with dead Sem and the unlucky Mongauli who had been hit by poison arrows or had their heads split by stone axe-blades. They lay where they had fallen. The injured were being brought to a field hospital set up near the middle of camp.

"It's odd," muttered Pollak suddenly as he looked around at the aftermath of the battle.

"What's odd, Pollak?"

"This attack. Don't you find it unusually reckless? I don't see the point."

"I do not, either. But I fear you may be overestimating the minds of these monkey wildlings."

"That may be. Still—"

"They don't think as you and I do, friend. Like a sand-worm, they strike by instinct at any enemy they come across. They are barbarians, nothing more."

"That is true, sir, but still it is strange to me." Pollak shook his head, a look of suspicion lingering on his face. Astrias laughed and asked him again what was strange about violent barbarians causing violence. But the young captain did not wait for the answer, for just then the flaps of the pavilion opened with a crisp snap, and the lady Amnelis showed herself outside for the first time since the attack began.

Because the pavilion had been erected on a slight rise, the general was visible from every part of the camp. Many gazed at her, for she was like a brilliant star on the morning horizon. The color rose to Astrias's cheeks, and he stared in awe at the vision of beauty.

Amnelis had equipped herself in full battle dress. She wore her white plate armor, high boots, and white fur cloak, above which her hair flowed freely like a shining waterfall of gold. The Nospherus sun shone down on her fair, noble face, and she lifted her left hand to shade her eyes. Standing there before the pavilion, the sunlight reflecting off her armor and hair, she had all the timeless beauty of a great painter's masterwork.

"What am I doing here? I must go report," said Astrias, his voice deep in his throat. He set out briskly toward his general as though drawn on a string. Pollak stayed behind, watching him go.

The other captains were already lined up before the pavilion and were beginning to give their reports.

"Irrim Corps. Dead: eight knights, thirty-four footmen. Wounded: two knights, eight footmen."

"Leegan Corps. None dead, none wounded."

Considering the amount of chaos following the surprise attack, the Mongauli losses were relatively light. Behind Amnelis, who stood with her hands on her hips listening to each captain's report in turn, a scribe furiously took down the numbers on a scroll of parchment.

"Astrias Corps. None dead, one light injury." When he had finished his report, Astrias stepped back and moved a little to one side, keeping his eyes fixed on Amnelis all the while.

While the reports continued, the Sem dead were counted. Two squads of Count Marus's knights that had been giving light chase to the fleeing Sem returned, having received strict orders not to follow the wildlings too deeply into the wilderness for fear of an ambush.

"We believe that no more than three hundred Sem have escaped," reported a squad leader of the blue knights who wore the crest of Tauride Castle. "We have confirmed approximately one hundred fifty Sem dead."

"Including the drummers and the ones making smoke, that means an attack force of around five hundred," said Amnelis, a look of disbelief on her face. "They sent a paltry five hundred warriors against our fifteen thousand?"

"General," said Count Marus, walking slowly up to the archduke's daughter.

"What is it, Marus?"

"Could this not be an attempt to draw us into pursuit?"

"They strike with five hundred, then immediately escape. We give chase and then their main force launches an attack. Yes, that is possible."

"Yet—" objected Irrim from the line of captains. "Yet even if all the Sem tribes were gathered together, they would find it difficult to match our numbers, General."

"True. Though it is hard to know their exact numbers, our reports suggest there are no more than ten thousand Sem in all Nospherus. Even if those reports were inaccurate, it is hard to imagine there being more than twice that number in this barren land."

"And, General, we know that the Sem tribes are divided. They often go to war with each other, slaying their own kind. I do not think that they could muster a force of any great size on short notice, and it has been only three days since we crossed the Kes."

"Then what possible reason could they have had to attack? With only five hundred warriors, it is as if they came to die."

The captains exchanged uncertain glances, but none among them could guess the import of that morning's battle. With the clever tactics they had used and the ferocity of their fighting, the Sem might have effectively capitalized on their advantage of surprise had there been as few as two thousand of them. But with only five hundred?

The number of Sem was far less than the Mongauli had imagined it to be during the battle, even after they had realized that the attacking force was relatively small. It made the invaders uneasy to wonder what the purpose of the assault might have been, what barbarian cunning might have led the Sem to attempt such an apparently foolhardy enterprise.

The meeting area in front of the pavilion was noisy with the captains' questions—questions without answers. Each commander gave his opinions loudly. Some thought that the wildlings had happened upon them, and that without thinking—for their brains were not equipped to handle the nuances of strategy—they had leapt to the assault, only to beat a hasty retreat when they found themselves hopelessly outnumbered.

Others believed that the attack had been a death squad sent to create a diversion, and that the main forces were waiting up ahead. That would explain why the Sem had been so intent on creating as much chaos as possible with their limited numbers, using smoke and drums to confuse the soldiers into believing that the wildlings were perhaps as numerous as the invaders. When their ruse was discovered, however, they had been forced to retreat to keep their losses as low as possible.

"Very odd…" muttered Count Marus, who had fallen back in line next to Astrias.

"What is it, Count?" Astrias inquired, remembering that Pollak had said the same thing. The venerable count glanced over at the younger man. Count Marus had been childhood friends with Astrias's father, Malks Astrias, who was now Lord Defender of Torus, commander of the capital's watch.

"How fare you, young Astrias?" The count turned and raised his hand genially, but there was a concerned look on his weathered face. "I find it very odd, this attack. I have fought with these barbarians many times in my years, but never have I seen them do something this…how shall I describe it?…this inexplicable. The attack this morning was unlike any Sem tactic I have ever seen. It worries me. I cannot say why I feel this, but I *do* feel that there was something strange about the Sem this morning. They were not the wildlings that I know. I fear that means they are planning something, but that in itself is odd, for I have seen many Sem ambushes and sneak attacks and the wildlings never seemed capable of high-level strategy.

"No, there is something amiss here, and we must be vigilant. We must not underestimate our enemy."

"Perhaps you should tell the Lady of Mongaul your concerns, Lord Count?" said Astrias, glancing over at Amnelis.

Count Marus joined him in gazing at their general. She had just finished some consultation with the diviner Gajus and was now motioning for silence.

"Knights of Mongaul, listen to me," she said in a voice high and clear. The captains were silent. "The Sem who attacked us have fled, but it appears that we are now in their territory. When we move, we must keep watch ahead and on both flanks at all times, and we must maintain our vigilance with the utmost keenness. Tell your men that from now on, when we pause to rest, they are to keep hold of their horses' tethers, and keep their scabbards loosened and their armor and helmets on at all times. We march in ten *shakes'* time. That is all."

The captains scattered, hurriedly making their way back to their troops. Astrias looked back at Count Marus, then glanced over to where Amnelis's retinue was busily dismantling the pavilion. Amnelis stood just before them, poring over the map of Nospherus, which was now spread out on the ground. Together with her two black-robed advisors, Gajus and the spellcaster Cal Moru, she was discussing their course. Astrias decided that it was an inopportune time to bring up the uncharacterstic behavior of the Sem. Quickly he made his way back to his men, for he had little time to prepare for the march.

Meanwhile, near the edge of the camp, two knights of the blue led by Count Marus were discussing lost property.

"Ye sure ye 'aven't seen me helmet, Guloran?"

"Nay, for the tenth time, nay. And that's eleven. This 'un's mine, right here where I left it, Tagg."

"Bloody thing! Where could it 'ave gone off ta?"

"What are you two quarreling about?"

"Ah, lieutenant, er, it's Tagg's helmet—he's lost it, he has."

"A helmet?" scoffed the lieutenant. "It was probably kicked away by some panicking horse. I'll make sure you get one from one of our dead. Now get ready, or you'll miss ranks when we muster. We're marching any moment now."

The soldier scratched his head perplexedly and grumbled a bit, but none of the others gave it much thought. Soon they would all forget about the lost helmet.

For, just moments later, the call to march went out, and the Mongauli army resumed its cautious advance.

Chapter Four

THE BATTLE OF NOSPHERUS

—— I ——

Even as the columns of the Mongauli army began to file, Guin, with the assistance of Loto of the Raku and Ilateli of the Guro, was busy leading the main force of the Sem far closer to the invaders than Amnelis and her captains would ever have guessed.

The Mongauli commanders were proceeding warily. With the early morning sneak attack fresh in their memories, they had assigned a generous number of scouts to sweep ahead of the advancing army, and the soldiers were alert and prepared for trouble as they began to march again. None among them dreamed that, even as their rear guard moved out of sight of the place where they had camped for the night, a force of five thousand Sem was gathering there.

As Count Marus had suspected, when the death squad of five hundred Sem attacked, the main force of five thousand wildlings was hiding nearby. For the Sem, who were born in

Nospherus and lived there their entire lives, the bleak wastelands that humankind knew only as a barren hell were neither
unexplored nor inhospitable. The rugged rocks and shifting
sands were entirely familiar to them; they knew the dangers of
the landscape and where they lay hidden. They knew in which
valleys the yidoh sprang, and in what hollows quicksand and
clusters of vampire moss lay. They were aware, too, of the valley
of death. It was the one place in their desert home where no
Sem would ever willingly set foot. They also knew of the oases,
where they were hidden and the distances between them. All
these things made up the first lesson each Sem child was taught
in its earliest days.

The Sem also knew that, in this place of vast empty horizons
where the eye could gaze across miles of unbroken barren
sands, there were in fact hidden river gorges, and secret caves
tunneled by the wind, and dunes that rose and fell and concealed narrow paths between them. They knew how to use the
features of the land to hide themselves, and now they used this
knowledge to sneak up as close as they could to the invading
army of Mongaul.

"What Riyaad said was true! The *oh-mu* look to the right,
and the left, and to the front, and up at the sky, but they believe
that behind them there is nothing but their own footprints,"
Siba, keen with pleasure, spoke from among the group of Sem

who stood close by Guin in the concealing shadow of a low out-crop of desert stone.

"Yes, Siba." Guin now wore a cloak with a long hood, made of cloth the color of sand, which he kept wrapped closely around himself to ensure that his golden head and mane were not by some chance spotted by the watchful eyes of the Mongauli. Gathered around him were the most important leaders of the force he had assembled: Loto, Ilateli, Tubai of the Tubai and Kalto of the Rasa, as well as the Crimson Mercenary Istavan of Valachia. The holy twins of Parros were there too, and so was inseparable little Suni.

"The death squad has returned, Riyaad," announced the young Raku who had been acting as their lookout. He had just hurried down from a high point on the outcrop.

"Are they not being followed by the *oh-mu*?" Loto asked worriedly.

Guin shook his head. "All is well. The squads they sent to pursue our force did not follow them far. I would guess that their commanders feared that a larger force might be hiding nearby, and told them not to give chase in earnest. Their army only began to march after all their cavalry had returned."

"It seems that is so, Riyaad."

The Sem death squad that had attacked the Mongauli camp earlier that morning had been made up of an even number of

Guro and Raku. In order to confuse any of the Mongauli who might attempt to follow them, they had followed a roundabout route in their flight, going well to the east before circling back around to rejoin the larger Sem army. They had been running at top speed the whole way, and they were out of breath as they arrived, desert-running Sem though they were.

"How many lost?" Guin inquired.

"One hundred thirty or forty, Riyaad."

"Less than a third. Still, I had hoped that the toll would be lighter. I had told them to withdraw after meeting our two objectives, but they must have gotten lost in the joy of battle."

"It was so."

The one who had led the death squad was Sebu of the Raku. He looked embarrassed.

"Well, it is unfortunate, but no matter. Did you succeed?"

"We did both things just as you said," Sebu told him, pulling out his spoils.

Guin looked them over carefully, and nodded.

"Good. Perfect. You got these, and you certainly achieved the other goal of confusing our enemies. By now, even as they hurry forward, the Mongauli are all wondering what the sneak attack was supposed to accomplish. After all, they are three times our number, and they know that if we do not proceed carefully we will be swallowed up in one gulp. And they know that we know this, too. So they wonder."

"Do we attack and finish them off now, Riyaad?" Ilateli asked impatiently. "If we catch up to them from the rear and kill a third of them with poison arrows, they will only be twice our number! We can kill another third with our stone axes, and they will be the same in number!"

"Before that happened, we, too, would be much reduced in number, and our situation would be no better," the leopard-man retorted, and gave a short laugh. Then he stood up with sudden catlike agility and continued, "No. We will not attack immediately, but we will not sit around all day, either. Our enemy certainly does not realize how close we are. They probably believe that a tribe living nearby happened upon them and foolishly attacked, then retreated in disarray. If so, we have a great advantage, an advantage that we must not squander."

"Hey, Rinda," whispered Remus. He was watching Guin, who had moved a few paces off and was now calling certain leaders of the Sem by name to gather around him. "Rinda, what do you think's going to happen?"

"How should I know?" Rinda snapped back.

Hearing her, Istavan came over to sit beside the two. "They're planning something totally crazy, Princess."

The mercenary squinted dubiously. Among those present, only he and the twins did not speak or understand the Sem language, so it often happened that, whether or not they got along, the three of them found themselves together.

"Totally crazy?" Rinda asked, led on by his words. Istavan often made her angry, but there was also something about the youth that made him almost impossible for her to ignore. The overly forward, self-proclaimed rapscallion of a mercenary possessed an infuriating sort of charisma.

"Yeah."

"And what, pray, is this totally crazy plan?"

"Well, you remember how in the dawn when we were leaving the Raku village, the monkeys were shouting about killing the Karoi?"

"Yes—and I was afraid they would proceed to do just that."

"And then Guin jumped up on that rock like Janos himself and gave his speech, and the monkeys, instead of saying 'kii kii' and waving their axes, finally calmed down a wee bit. By the end, they were yelling 'Riyaad! Riyaad!' I wondered what leopard-head had said to them to calm them down, so I asked him on our way from the Raku valley to this—what's it called?—yes, 'night-wailing-rock hill.'"

"And what had Guin told them?"

"Well, that's just it." Istavan drew out the moment, enjoying the chance to bait her impatience by pretending to withhold something important. "To hear Guin tell it, he didn't say anything special to them. He just told them that we have a chance to win. And why? Because we have a secret weapon, a powerful ally that can turn the odds of ten-and-five thousand versus five thousand on its head. That was his answer. So I asked him what in the name of Jarn he had in mind. And then…"

"Yes?"

"That leopard-headed madman gave one of his howling laughs and answered, 'Nospherus!' I asked him what he meant by that, but he wouldn't tell me. All he said was that he'd told the Sem that, before another day passes, the Karoi will join us anyways. Can you believe it?"

"The Karoi?" Rinda's eyes became round. "I don't understand. The Karoi cut off the Raku messengers' heads, and said unkind things."

"Hey, it wasn't me that said the Karoi would join us. You'll have to talk to Guin if you don't believe me, and good luck trying to get *him* to explain anything." Istavan's dusky face made a frown. "I'm sure he's got some plan. By Doal, I'm sure that, thanks to his plan, I'll end up dumped on some dung heap this time."

"Why do you say that?"

Istavan didn't answer, but instead said something so lewd that not only Rinda's but Remus's face turned bright red.

Just as Rinda was about to harangue the mercenary for not watching his tongue, Guin bellowed, "Istavan! Come here."

Guin had gathered the Sem chieftains, and they were working out some complicated plan. It seemed that some part of
their planning was already finished, and the leaders of the
Tubai and the Rasa ran off to gather their tribesmen.

"Istavan!"

"All right, I'm coming! Hey, Guin, are you sure I have to…
you know, what you said earlier?"

A disgruntled Istavan ambled reluctantly over to where
Guin was standing. The leopard-man drew back his sand colored hood and laughed his short fierce laugh.

"I am sorry, there is no one else to do it. Neither I, nor the
children, nor any of the Sem could fill that role."

"Doalspit! Why do I always get the short straw?" Istavan
grumbled, then muttered a string of lewd curses under his
breath. Guin paid him no attention.

"If we have a chance to win, it is this: we must divide the
Mongauli army. It is too large for us now, but if we can split
them into groups of as few as possible, we can improve our
odds. There may be fifteen thousand of them, but divide them,
and we will be facing three groups of five thousand, or seven
groups of only twenty hundred each."

"I know, I know. I understand your madman's logic. I'll do
it, okay? Does that cheer you up?"

Guin nodded. Then, he began to give detailed instructions

to the sulking mercenary. Their low voices were not audible to the twins, who were sitting a short distance away so as not to be in the way of the many chieftains.

The heir to the throne of Parros was gazing thoughtfully at the two warriors. "I wonder what Guin's planning."

"I don't know," Rinda replied dreamily. "But I think that, for now, we'll be okay if we leave everything up to him. I sense it, and that's all I know. Oh, Remus, what a man Guin is! I've never met anyone like him! It's not just his appearance, of course. The more I get to know him, the less I believe someone like him really exists!" Rinda's face was glowing. In her eyes was the gleam of pride and revelation of a fervent worshipper. Her brother peered at her, and agreed cautiously.

"What!" Istavan cried.

Surprised, the two twins turned to look at him, and even Suni, who had been gazing up with reverence at Rinda's face, stared at the mercenary.

"Quiet, Istavan," Guin growled.

Istavan was outraged by something that the leopard-man had just said. "How can you say it just like that, like we were talking about someone else?" he demanded. "You're asking *me*? What do you think I am? Okay, I understand, I'll do it. I'll bleeding do it. Fine. By the pimples on Jarn's bristly hide, I've come this far, I'll do anything, you damn leopard-head."

All at once the mercenary tore off his armor and threw it down on the ground, leaving himself mostly naked. Remus's eyes went round. Rinda's face blushed pure red, and she turned away.

Indifferent to his royal audience, Istavan pulled off his black shirt, socks and breeches. Then, wearing only his dark suntan, the muscular mercenary stuck out his hand with something like abandon. "Okay, give it to me. Give it to me quick before I catch a cold."

The sun was already quite high in the deep violet sky of the no-man's-land. Below it, stretching out like a fair spring mist above a river valley, was a low white cloud. It was a cloud of risen dust, and it heralded the advance of the Mongauli army.

Only three *twists* after beginning their march, the Mongauli army had slowed abruptly at a warning signal from its outriders.

"Report! Report!"

The ranks of the Gohran soldiers hurriedly parted on either side to admit the returning scouts.

"Report! Report!"

The scouts sped into the group of white knights at the very center of the formation, and orders immediately went out to the front and rear of the army. With the precision borne of long training, the entire force halted.

"All troops, as you are."

Captains' voices shouted back and forth, adjusting the formation.

"Scouts, approach." Amnelis, gazing out sternly from the saddle of her great white charger, removed her helm as she waited for her outriders to proceed.

"I have a report, my lady." A knight who had been scouting to the northeast bowed nervously before the general.

"Do not waste time on formalities. Speak!"

"A large army of the Sem is approaching from our left rear flank."

"What?" Amnelis's lips tightened. "And their number?"

"Unknown, my lady, but I believe it is quite a large army. The dust rises up in a towering wall."

Without thinking, the knights who had heard this turned to gaze in the direction of which he spoke. Worry crept into their hearts. Across a large stretch of desert there they could see the pale gray dust rising in a haze.

"Distance?"

"Around three tads, I believe."

Amnelis's expression was stern. "You have done well, soldier, now return to the main force," she nodded to the scout. Then she glanced quickly over her shoulder.

"Feldrik!"

"Yes, my lady!"

"Orders!"

"Yes, my lady!"

"Gather all the officers, lieutenants and up."

"Yes, my lady!"

Feldrik, who was in charge of the messengers of the white, sped to his gathered knights.

"Orders! Orders!"

Again the whole Mongauli army waited in tense anticipation.

"The Sem are attacking!"

"It's an attack!"

The cries passed from mouth to mouth, spreading like wildfire through the ranks.

"Gajus," Amnelis spoke in a low voice to the caster.

"Yes?"

"What do you think? Is this the main Sem army, for which the sneak attack was a diversion?"

"You ask my opinion?"

"They tested us with a small force, then maneuvered to outflank us, and are now attacking from behind, correct?"

"Yes, that is what I believe."

"So this time it will not be a mere squabble."

"I believe not, my lady."

"Gajus."

"Yes?"

"There is one thing that bothers me still. They must have learned how many we are during their sneak attack this morning. Could the Nospherus Sem be so innumerable that they outnumber us?"

"I am unsure…"

"Very well, then divine whether we will win or lose with your board and sphere. And once the battle is joined, I want you to make sure that our guide to the Valley of Death is not lost. You must protect Cal Moru and our compass."

"As you wish," replied the dark runecaster.

Without looking at him again, Amnelis gave her horse a quick flick of her whip and wheeled to ride before the officers who had hastily assembled at her orders. Vlon and Lindrot, who bore her flag high, followed behind her.

"Report!"

A second band of scouts had returned. Amnelis delayed issuing her orders.

"I have seen the Sem! The wildling army is ten thousand strong! They are about two and a half tads behind our formation and are approaching at full speed."

"Well done," Amnelis said.

Irrim, captain of the black, muttered, "The Sem are swift-footed little creatures. I can see why they are called the snakes of the desert."

Tangard responded in a whisper, "Their legs *are* fast—as fast as horses—and they can run for great stretches of time."

"Silence!" Amnelis admonished, raising her right hand. "We have heard the report of our enemies' strength! Are you listening? The Sem forces are estimated at around ten thousand. We will meet them and crush them here and now. Our vanguard—"

The young Astrias and Irrim stepped forward, hoping to be chosen for the most dangerous position. Amnelis looked at both men briefly.

"Irrim!"

"Yes, my lady!"

"Send your bowmen up front, and set them in crescent formation."

"Yes, my lady!"

The vice-lord of Talos Keep spurred his horse's flanks and headed off. Astrias followed him with his eyes, his envy manifest.

"Tangard!"

"Yes, my lady!"

"Your footmen will support Irrim as necessary. Otherwise ensure that all our central positions and baggage train are defended...

"Marus, you will take the rear!"

"Yes, my lady!"

"Leegan take the left, Astrias the right!"

"Yes, General!"

"Each knightly corps shall position bowmen at the front. Behind them, line up your shield wall and your footmen. The cavalry shall be staged hindmost, poised for a counterattack. When you charge with your horses, keep their heads down so the Sem arrows don't get into their eyes."

"Yes, my lady!"

"Stay alert!"

Each of the captains galloped away, followed by their lieutenants. Soon all were busy with the complex task of ordering their troops into position.

Once more the brilliant four-colored flower bloomed in the desert. This time, however, it was a misshapen, irregular bloom, with two red petals stuck out like horns on either side, while the center grew thicker and the top took the shape of a bristling crescent.

The squads of bowmen moved to the front of the ranks. Each of these soldiers dropped to one knee and readied his weapon so that at the order they could send a volley of shot flying. Behind each formation of bowmen, a row of wooden shields was set to ward off the Sem's poison arrows. The spears of the footmen formed a forest behind them. At the rear of the ranks, mounted troops rubbed their horses' necks and held their reins tightly to keep them under control.

A third group of scouts came racing in through the crescent formation of Irrim's bowmen and between lifted shields, galloping toward the general. "Their vanguard is closing in!" they shouted.

In the right wing, Pollak, the second-in-command, sat easy on his horse, his scabbard loosened so that he could draw at any moment. "Captain," he called to Astrias.

"What?"

"Getting put on the right wing—boring, eh?"

"The Lady General knows best," Astrias shrugged. "Don't worry, there are lots coming this time. I'm sure we will have plenty of sport all along the lines."

"I'm not worried," Pollak laughed, an eager light in his eyes.

Astrias turned to assure himself that his troops were not lacking in morale, and indeed no face he saw was pale from the winds of cowardice. Then, with hands encased in chainmail gauntlets, he drew the cord around his leather neckpiece, fastening his helmet securely on his head. The red plume fixed at the top of his helm shimmered and flowed like fire when he moved his head. With a snap he lowered his faceplate.

"Very well, let them come!" he muttered fiercely, and his body shook in anticipation of the coming fight.

The Mongauli troops knew how to take orders and had

moved swiftly into position. Now, each warrior at his post, the great invasion force braced for the Sem onslaught. Like a thunder cloud of ill omen bearing a terrible rain, the yellow-gray billow of dust thrown up from the dry soil of Nospherus was approaching at what seemed to be ever-increasing speed.

"They come!" Astrias heard somebody, perhaps Pollak, shout.

"Ah, there's a whole lot of 'em," another knight grunted.

Grimly the Mongauli waited. Now all the crossbows were cranked and loaded with shot, and all of them aimed at the rapidly slithering thundercloud. Each knight laid his right hand on the grip of his long sword, and each left hand grasped the reins of a stamping horse.

The flag-bearers around Amnelis formed a core of pure white defended by thick bastions of black, blue, and red. Motionless, the lady-general gazed upon the battlefield.

Suddenly she raised her hand, and, as though she had unexpectedly found it hard to breathe, she lifted open her faceplate. Her gaze was intense and her fair visage was drawn tight as she looked toward the approaching cloud.

Amnelis was only just eighteen and a woman among hard-bitten warrior men. Yet, having fought in her first battle at age fifteen, she had taken up a sword many times since, leading in the field as a commander and waging wars as a general. Now she was the supreme General of the Right, a formidable fighter and a veteran of many campaigns.

The yellow-and-ash dust cloud grew bigger and bigger in the eyes of all the Mongauli. Still staring at it, Amnelis hesitated, then took off her helmet entirely and let her golden hair flow down over her shoulders.

"It is dangerous to expose your face, my lady," Feldrik cautioned her immediately.

She silenced him with her left hand, and made as though to listen to something. Low, and with surprise in her voice, she said, "It is quiet, is it not?"

At that very moment there came the whiz of a lone arrow flying through the air. As though it were a signal, it was followed a moment later by a fearsome cacophony.

"Aiiie!"

"Ayyyy ayyy ayy!"

"Iieeee ieee iee!"

Sem war cries sounded in the ears of the Mongauli host.

"The enemy!"

"They attack!"

From all four sides there came the roar of war, and the battle was joined in earnest.

2

"Listen, Sem—Raku, Guro, Tubai, Rasa!"

Not long before the battle with the Gohran invaders began, Guin was repeating his orders to the wildlings. The ape-men were unused to fighting together as a group, and he admonished them sternly.

"You must not spread out and divide your forces! We do not have the numbers for such careless tactics. Your enemies are trained elites. If they learn how few we are, then we are done for. Lose yourself in the heat of battle, and forget what I have said, and that will be the end of the Sem!"

"Aiii!"

The brave Sem warriors brandished their stone axes and stone-tipped spears.

"Riyaad! Riyaad!"

"Do you understand? You must do exactly as I have told you!"

Istavan was nowhere to be seen among the assembled Sem, nor the twins Rinda and Remus. In fact, the wildling army he spoke to seemed considerably smaller than the force of five thousand that the grand alliance of Sem tribes—excluding only the two thousand Karoi—had placed at Guin's disposal.

The Mongauli scouts, judging the numbers of the Sem by the dust cloud they raised, would report to their general that ten thousand of the diminutive warriors were approaching them. But here were gathered less than half that number.

"Are you ready? This will not be the final battle, but how we do today may determine the ultimate victor. Don't forget that. Remember my orders and don't let them know our true numbers. Kick your feet and raise a giant cloud of dust!"

Guin rode atop an enormous black stallion that one of the Sem chieftains had procured for him. Upon it, he looked like an avatar of the beast-god Sasaidon leading a war party of little demons, or some giant-king of myth and magic leading the spirit folk of the earth.

Lifting his right hand high and bringing it down in a chopping motion, Guin gave the signal to begin the attack, and the Sem began to move as one.

The leopard-man had divided the Sem into four groups of a little less than a thousand each. Led by Loto, Ilateli, Tubai, and Kalto, each of these mixed forces now advanced in the shape of a slender triangle with its sharpest point forward. They held this formation until, still shrouded in their dust cloud, they were almost in sight and range of the Mongauli army with its bowmen at the forefront waiting for the order to shoot. Then the battalions of Sem began a peculiar maneuver.

They advanced to just the range at which their poison arrows became effective. The four battalions then began to circle like the arms of a pinwheel, shooting poison arrows toward the Mongauli army as they revolved. As soon as one group fired, it swiftly swung around to the right and gave up its place to the next.

This was a tactic Guin had adopted to mislead the enemy further about the Sem's numbers. On a flat plain with the opposing forces at a considerable distance from each other, unlike in a siege, missile weapons were of limited use. Neither Gohran bowshot nor Sem arrow had their full devastating effect. The Sem's poisoned arrows, fired at long range, were easily knocked aside, or bounced off helmets and armor. Bowshot, on the other hand, was extremely slow to load, and did not always serve as more than a means of intimidation.

The opening salvos were about to come to an end.

"Bowmen, stop shooting!"

"Footmen, advance!"

With these orders, the Mongauli crossbowmen started to

withdraw, and footmen clad in shiny armor removed the shield wall. Then, brandishing their spears, the infantry companies of Talos began their advance.

Seeing this change of tactics on the part of their enemies, the Sem put away their bows. Drawing their stone axes and raising their terrifying war cries, the wildling warriors charged for the front lines of the Mongauli.

"Aii, Iiaa!"

"Riyaad! Riyaad!"

"Aii ai ai!"

Against the birdlike calls of the Sem sounded the full-throated pledges of the human troops.

"For Mongaul!"

"Mongaul! Mongaul!"

"Forward, brave warriors! Forward!"

The advancing troops were clad in black. Captain Irrim was the vice-lord of Talos Keep, one of the five Marches strongholds, and he had defended against many a Sem attack during his tenure. Now he shouted with wild courage to inspirit his men.

Irrim was baffled by the strange yet precisely organized movements of the Sem, for he was unaccustomed to seeing the barbarians of Nospherus employ sophisticated tactics. In every past battle with the ape-men, he had known them simply to shoot their poison arrows haphazardly, before raising a chorus of strange yells and charging in wildly. The vice-lord of Talos knew how to respond to such an attack.

It seemed to him that the large force currently arrayed against him was behaving entirely differently. This Sem army was now sending well-knit troop after troop in lightning-like advances, each approaching from the right to attack, only to retreat away to the left, to be replaced immediately by another fresh troop that would repeat the maneuver. The endless waves made the wildlings' numbers difficult to estimate. They seemed to have an unending supply of fresh forces, striking and then running away.

"The monkeys have learned some trick!"

Irrim bit his lip and pounded his gauntlet on the hard edge of his saddle, leaning forward to shout encouragements to his men. "Don't be fooled by their movements! Close ranks, and stand your ground! We must not shame the lord of Talos Keep by accepting reinforcements! Fight! Fight!"

"Aiii!"

"Iiaaa!"

The battle was reaching a ferocious pitch. The high wild screams and moans of the wounded and the violent clangor of sword blade and stone axe striking home began to drown out even the fiercest of the battle cries.

"Aaaah!" the commander of black knights exclaimed in shock. "What is that thing?!"

Captain Irrim had been distracted from his assessment of Sem tactics by a new and terrible sight. Riding into the fray at the head of a fresh band of Sem was a formidable lone knight who seemed impossibly huge among his wildling cohorts.

Irrim leaned over the knob of his saddle and stared in his shock, having lost his voice. Who was he? He was no Sem. Could he even be called human? *By the gods, it's a man with the head of a leopard!*

Perched effortlessly atop his mighty black charger, glistening with the sweat and blood of battle and surrounded by his legions of fanatical Sem, Guin cut a figure that no other could hope to equal. To the eyes of the Mongauli, who expected only the small fur-covered wildlings with their shrill shouts and their painted faces and hands, the fascinating sight of a leopard-headed warrior seemed almost like an irresistible illusion. Guin, clad only in a loincloth and sword belt, his broad chest rippling with muscle as he swung his sword, drove all before him.

"Janos save us! Who, or what, is that?"

"It's Cirenos! The legendary Cirenos, that's who it is!"

"Ah, how he fights! Look!"

Irrim and the black knights of Talos Keep were some of

those who had crossed over the Kes in the second wave and had joined the expeditionary force midway. Few among them had heard of the man-beast whose figure had stupefied the brave knights of Alvon and Stafolos.

Yet now they were faced with an amazing warrior who wielded his sword with movements far more agile than his size ought to have allowed. Charging into the wavering lines, he cut down Mongauli soldiers effortlessly on either side. None could stand against him. Whenever that sword flashed, a dead man always fell.

The battle lines fell into chaos. The Sem army, too, was caught up in the madness of the melee, and now they fell on the human lines as one mass as though they had forgotten their axle-turning strategem. But since the arrayed black knights, captivated by Guin, had surrendered all semblance of order, Irrim and his officers failed to perceive that there were in fact only thirty hundred or so Sem arrayed against them. The leopard-headed warrior's movements inexorably drew the eyes of friend and foe alike.

Guin by himself fought and brought death with the power of a dozen Sem, if not an entire troop of them. Although he wore not a single piece of armor, the frequently drilled warriors of Mongaul could not even touch him, even when they attacked in groups of ten. Time and again the flashing sword in his right hand reached out, and time and again Mongauli blood was spilled.

"Stand firm, soldiers! Do not flee! He is only one, this enemy!" Irrim, who at first had been just as entranced as the others by the unexpected appearance of this fearsome demigod, had finally returned to his senses, and now he ground his teeth and yelled. "Surround him! Surround him with many, cut him down! If we can kill that one monster, there will only be barbarians left, who cannot hope to match us! Ach, I'm going in!"

Irrim beat on his saddle and drove his heels against his horse's sides, fully meaning to gallop into the thick of battle, but his aides hastily cut off his approach to the fighting.

The fact that things were not going well for the troops from Talos was apparent to the two young captains of the red positioned each in his wing. But when the leopard-headed warrior, not even wearing a mantle, charged into the maelstrom of battle, one of the two captains from Alvon raised himself up in his saddle with a start.

"Ah!" It was Astrias, who had suffered horrible defeat at the hands of Guin and the Raku not long ago. "It's him!"

"I have a message for your lady general who fights and commands like a man. Leave the wildlings and the creatures of Nospherus alone..."

So Guin had told him, coldly, as the young captain lay

overthrown. Then the leopard-man had pulled back the sword he held at Astrias's throat. It was a memory that filled the Red Lion of Gohra with a stew of shame, anger, and resentment. His face went almost blue with fury.

"Pollak!"

"It is him, is it not? Look at his strength!" Pollak's voice was trembling slightly.

"Gahhh!" Astrias yelled. "Monster!" And with that cry, the Red Lion of Gohra charged ahead.

"Captain!" Pollak, realizing that his commander had lost his cool, tried to stop him, but he was not quick enough.

The sight of Guin once more dealing destruction before his eyes rendered irrelevant for Astrias his position as the leader of a thousand knights, and the general's strict orders not to charge until so commanded. "I shall be the one to stop him!" he shouted, and dug his heels into his horse's sides with all the force he could muster. The bewildered steed galloped into the fray at full speed, weaving between the Sem and the footmen from Talos.

"No!" shouted Pollak. "Save the captain! Astrias Corps, forward!"

In an instant the entire right wing had abandoned its assigned task of protecting one of the flanks of the army.

Leegan, commander of the left wing, was taken aback.

"What? Has there been an order to send in the wings?"

His lieutenant Len, no less confused, replied, "Ah, no—there has not been. At least, I do not think so."

"That is odd. Astrias Corps has gone to aid the Talos footmen. Why would only one wing receive the order to charge? Len, send a rider at once to Lady Amnelis and ask what our orders are. In the meantime, I will join this battle myself and see what's going on. It won't do to let Astrias take all the glory for himself!"

Astrias, scion of a leading house of Torus, and Leegan, the eldest son of Count Ricard, keep-lord of Alvon, were both viscounts and nearly the same age. Good friends since their youngest days, they had always been in competition as such boys are wont to be. Seeing Astrias join the fight, Leegan was spurred on. From the beginning he had been trembling with anticipation and had a sour taste in his mouth at having been sentenced to wing duty.

"Are you sure that is wise, without the general's permission?" Len cautioned.

"I don't care! Quickly, send a soldier to her and ask. Ech, never mind, we're going in!" Abruptly, he raised his hand and whipped his horse, and the thousand red knights of Alvon that he led charged forth.

Astrias was already in the midst of the fighting.

"Guin! Fight me, Guin! I challenge you! What, are you scared? Guin!" he roared and cut a road of blood, making for the leopard-headed warrior who was slashing back and forth amidst a group of Mongauli warriors. "Yaaar—I have no business with you monkeys!" Astrias knocked away the Sem to his left and right with the butt of his whip. "Have you forgotten me? Or are you just a coward, Guin? Here I am! I, Astrias, challenge you!" Soon his throat was hoarse with shouting.

It was Irrim who was the most surprised by the movement of the red knigths. "What? Young Astrias? Was he commanded to save us? Troops! Captain Astrias has been sent to aid you! This will bring shame on Talos for a generation! What is wrong with you? Have you forgotten how to use your blades? Finish off those monkeys and that monster, quick!" As he shouted, he noticed a white knight making his way forward through the ranks. He bore a blue flag on his spear and wore the tassel of the messenger on his shoulder.

"Where is Lord Irrim?" the messenger shouted.

"Here, over here!" shouted the commander of the black.

"I have orders. The leopard-headed warrior who leads the Sem holds the key to a valuable secret. You are not to kill him, but to take him alive. I repeat, he must not be harmed! This is a direct order from the general."

"Understood," Irrim grumbled. But after the messenger

was gone, he exclaimed in exasperation, "How am I to take alive the living Cirenos? Do they think I own the legendary net of Kaurinos? Not do him any harm!"

He raised his faceplate and spat on the ground, then turned to his lieutenant. "Lukas—deliver those orders! Right now!"

The lieutenant hurriedly galloped into the fray.

Meanwhile, Astrias, in the thick of the battle, was in no mood to pay attention to any order not to do harm. Even had he learned of such a command from the lady-general, he was so caught up in his burning rage and shame that he would have disregarded it.

Now, Guin, I have found you!

The leopard-man towered like an immovable pillar in the midst of a pile of corpses clad in black armor. He was drenched in the blood of his enemies, painted pure red from the top of his round, inhuman head to the ragged loincloth at his waist; his broad chest was like a map of hell defined by his own mountainous muscles. The great sword in his hand was barely recognizable as such, clotted as it was from its hilt to its tip in Mongauli gore.

For a moment, the horrifying force of his heroic rage had frightened off all who would oppose him. He was waiting in the lull for the next wave of opponents, taking stock of his situation. It was into this lull that Astrias came galloping.

"Guin! You were lucky once to beat me—me, Astrias, the Red Lion of Gohra. You made me retreat in shame. This grudge I bear, but I will remove it now! Meet me! Fight me!" the young captain shouted at the top of his lungs. But when Guin turned and looked at him, a sudden chill came over his body and all his hair stood on end.

Guin's eyes let off a light that was amazing, yellow, burning like an inferno. Here was no human warrior but a giant blood-covered beast, drenched in the ichor of the humans he had destroyed and devoured, a mage-beast, greatly to be feared. An enlightenment of terror pierced Astrias like a thunderbolt.

He wavered and hesitantly backed his horse away—then stopped, chagrined and even angrier than before.

"FIGHT ME, GUIN!" he screamed, pouring all the strength he could into this challenge. He brandished his sword and prepared to charge, but just then, Guin smiled—or rather, although the leopard mask remained as expressionless as always, it seemed to Astrias that Guin was smiling wryly at him. Perhaps the light in those eyes, a man-eating leopard's eyes, softened just a little, the fearsome glint that moments before would have made a weak man drop dead of shock.

"You are no challenge for me, little one. Wait twenty years and come again. Then I will fight you," Guin replied in his characteristic growl, and turned to survey the battlefield. All at once the leopard warrior returned from his battle rage to cold rationality. "Damn! The Sem have lost themselves in the battle," Guin muttered in a voice so low none heard him.

Then, without even looking at Astrias, who waited nearby, too overcome by his awesome enemy's presence now even to breathe, the leopard-man spurred his horse back into the conflict.

"Siba! Siba!"

"Yes, Riyaad!"

"Retreat—blow your whistle!"

"Yes, Riyaad!"

Siba took up the bamboo whistle that hung at his throat and blew with all his might. Guin charged down the battle lines on his horse, seeking Ilateli and Loto. "Retreat! Don't forget the plan!" he yelled sternly.

From here and there sounded the high pitched whistles of the Sem, one adding to the other. Though they had seemed lost in their battle rage, the wildlings managed to remember Guin's master plan and their wits returned to them.

"Aii Aii Aii!"

"Iia Iia Iiiia!"

"Aiiaa, Aiii!"

Howling now like mountain wolves, the Sem began a rapid retreat.

"Don't let them escape! Give chase!" shouted Irrim.

The Mongauli under his command made to move but stopped in their tracks. Guin, the mad warrior who had driven them all over the brink of terror, was now returning, followed by a contingent of Sem barbarians. The leopard-man drew up before the breathless troops of men and his voice roared out like thunder.

"Lady General of Mongaul, the Sem challenge you!"

Thrusting his arm back, he lofted a spear he had taken from one of the footmen—over Irrim's head, toward the troop of white knights who were arrayed around Amnelis.

The spear flew with incredible force, and Vlon moved swiftly to push Amnelis out of its path. A moment later, in the place where she had stood, the weapon sank deep into the earth, its long haft wobbling back and forth.

"Aaaa!" the lady-general screamed. She covered her mouth in surprise and her cheeks flushed the color of blood, the same color as the Nospherus evening sun.

How could I let the soldiers hear me cry out like a little girl!

Into Amnelis's ears, which had turned bright red with her embarrassment, came a fearless laugh and a booming voice. "May that be a lesson for you! Go home and lengthen the hem of your dress, and spend your time turning men's heads in the temple ballroom! It would suit you far better, tomboy general!"

"...!"

It was as though the entire army had gasped.

Then, before any could react, the blood-covered demon-god had whirled about like a desert wind and galloped off after the retreating Sem forces.

"Follow him…" Amnelis's voice croaked. Her words were barely audible, so overcome was she with rage. She placed her hand on her chest, and licked her lips many times. Only then could she shout piercingly, "Give chase! Do not let a single Sem soldier survive! Follow them! Follow!"

"All troops, charge!"

The Mongauli army hastily reorganized and began pursuing the Sem, who were taking a northwesterly course.

Although the Irrim Corps had suffered serious losses in the battle, it too moved to advance, heedless of their wounded and dead, let alone those of the Sem. Still, order came for the Irrim Corps to fall back into the center of the formation, and it switched places with Tangard's contingent.

The Mongauli army changed shape. The ends of the loose crescent curved upwards as both wings set out in advance. The invaders were moving to the attack in the shape of a great U. Astrias, back at the head of his own corps, led his red knights in the forefront, whipping his horse to increase its speed. His face was pale.

You…you you you!

If his men could have seen his young face under his face-plate, or if they could have heard the silent curses rolling off his tongue, they would have realized to their astonishment that their captain, only twenty years of age but already famous and formidable, was crying. Astrias's tears were tears of burning fury. The rage he felt that hour he would never forget for his whole life thereafter.

There was one other in that army who was also crying bitter, unseen tears—none other than the Lady of Mongaul herself.

And so, directed by rage and frustration, the Mongauli army undertook its pursuit of the Sem. Already, the invaders had completely ceased to watch their back and flanks.

—— 3 ——

The Mongauli army continued its pursuit of the fleeing Sem.

The sun was high in the sky, soaking the white ash of the wastelands with harsh white light, casting small, dark shadows under the knights' horses. The troops rode fast and no longer in formation; their columns had stretched into long lines, and in places, no more than two or three rode abreast. It seemed to them as if the battle with the Sem had gone on forever, but in truth the entire conflict had lasted no more than a *twist*.

At the front of the lines, the captains shouted their throats sore in the rising dust.

"Give chase!"

"Don't let them get away!"

Only half a tad or so ahead of the leading knights rode Guin, with Siba and a thousand of the other Sem warriors running fast on their short legs behind him. They looked like a phantasm born of a desert mirage, Guin riding his massive black steed across the barren waste, the Sem flowing behind him like a wild tide across the parched ground. Truly, it was a scene out of legend. Guin kept strict control of his steed, slowing the great stallion so that he would not leave Siba and his band behind. The blood that covered his muscled body was now streaked with runnels of sweat as the high Nospherus sun beat down upon him. His mask glistened crimson and gold.

"Siba! How fare you?" the leopard-man yelled back over the sound of pounding hooves and pattering feet.

"Riyaad! We all follow you!"

The shouts of the Mongauli army came to them from behind, carried on the desert winds.

"Stop them! Stop them!"

"Don't let them escape!"

"Keep up the chase!"

Guin growled. "Siba! We have almost reached the first landmark."

"Yes, Riyaad!"

"Then it is time!"

As he ran, Siba stuck a hand deep into a bag at his waist and brought out a small, round fruit. Holding it over his head, he covered his nose and mouth with his other hand and screwed his eyes shut. Then with great force he crushed the fruit in the air above him.

There was a slight cracking sound, and a burst of juice spilled out in a surprising gush from the small fruit, soaking his head and neck and trickling down to his waist.

Siba howled. The juice stank powerfully of ammonia, its fumes spreading out behind him in a great cloud. All around him, the other Sem pulled out similar fruits and administered the same foul baptism to themselves. In moments, the Sem troop was transformed into an almost comical band of red-eyed warriors, weeping and coughing at the stench. Yet they did not slow their pace in the least.

Siba looked up through tearing eyes and noticed a change in the scenery around them. "Riyaad, we will soon reach the Devil's Anvil!"

"Good! Then we must run faster, brave Sem!" howled Guin. He raised his horsewhip and brought it down hard on his steed's flank. Though bewildered by the stench all around it, the horse responded to this harsh treatment with another burst of speed. The Sem pounded across the loose sand to keep pace.

The Devil's Anvil was an area of hard white sand, baked by the sun during the day and cold and exposed during the night. It lay lower and flatter than the surrounding desert. Guin, sitting tall on his horse, was the first to see it as they arrived to its edge. The desert before him seemed to boil, and all at once he could make out the shapes of a giant colony of yidoh. They were the same white color as the sand, lying flat under the baking rays of the sun. They seemed to cover the entire expanse of the Anvil in a white sea of jelly, trembling, waiting for some unwitting prey to come and ease their blind, eternal hunger.

Guin and Siba's band were charging right into their midst! Instantly, the yidoh rose, disturbed by the intrusion, and began to undulate toward them. It was a hellish sight, one that would chill the blood of the strongest warrior in an instant.

Guin's eyes grew bloodshot and the short hairs on the back of his neck stood on end. His strong body broke out in goose bumps, reacting with natural instincts of fear and disgust that even a warrior such as he could not suppress. Siba and the others were similarly affected. Their faces contorted with fear, pants and curses tumbled from their mouths. Yet when the yidoh that had surged toward them caught the scent of the yidoh-bane that the warriors had spread upon themselves, the shapeless monsters recoiled violently, pulling back like a receding tide and forcing their cousins who gathered behind them even further back. Thus a path was opened for Guin's mad dash, as if he were some improbable prophet and the living sea had parted before him.

Yet the racing warriors had a long distance to cover to cross the Anvil, and the Nospherus sun shone down mercilessly upon them. Soon its beams had dried and evaporated the juice of the alika plant which they had squeezed over themselves to ward off the yidoh.

Siba thrust his hand into his bag again, and, grimacing, he broke another alika fruit above his head, showering himself once more with its noxious juice. The Sem behind him followed suit, and Guin squeezed two alikas in his powerful hands, dripping their juice down onto his horse's forelegs.

Yet these were the last of the fruits they had carried with them. If this juice dried, the hurrying troop would be left defenseless in the middle of the sea of yidoh, and theirs would be an unspeakably horrible death.

Now fear settled upon them, making their throats tighten and their legs go weak. Already they imagined the dread sensation of their bodies being absorbed by those sticky, slimy creatures, and they ran for dear life. The Devil's Anvil seemed to stretch out forever before them, and, natural desert runners though they were, the Sem found their breath coming ragged, and their shoulders heaved desperately.

At last they saw what they had been hoping to see.

"Quick, this way!"

"Riyaad! You are safe!"

It was the women of the Tubai, apparently standing knee-deep in the endless sea of yidoh, right there at the far end of the Devil's Anvil. They held long staves in their hands, which they waved at Guin's party. Swiftly Guin's force turned to approach them, and as they did, the Tubai women took their long, strangely shaped staves and thrust them out into the boiling yidoh. The yidoh quickly parted to either side. Led by the staff-wielding women, the fighting force swiftly passed through the rest of the yidoh colony upon the Anvil.

The Tubai women gathered around them. They were dressed strangely, legs sheathed in bark moccasins that rose up to their knees, and hats on their heads also made of tree bark. From the belts at their waists many black fruits hung by threads, and from their furry hands and feet came the strong smell of ammonia, an odor that also emanated from the staves in their hands and spread across a wide area around them.

All that they wore and carried was made out of alika wood: the shoes, the hats, the staves, and even the belts which bore the alika fruits. The Tubai were also known as the yidoh-kin, for they did not fear the horrible yidoh of Nospherus, but rather herded and used them. They knew how to control the creatures' movements and raised them in the middle of alika groves, the very thing that yidoh hated more than anything else.

"We did as you said!"

"Will this be enough, Riyaad?" the women asked, clustered close to Guin. The leopard-man stood among them like a father surrounded by his children and nodded, looking out at the sea of yidoh.

"Very well, this is enough for now."

"We've never gathered this many together at one time before. We feared that we'd run out of alika fruit!"

"I think half the yidoh in Nospherus might be here," said another.

The Tubai women laughed like delighted children.

The sea of yidoh that buried the wide Devil's Anvil ended at the edge of that flat place. Beyond it, the ground was rockier, and among those rocks the main force of Sem now waited, the warriors resting their tired bodies.

"Riyaad." Loto came running up.

"How is it with our troops? What are our losses?"

"They are not so severe as they might have been, Riyaad. Well under a thousand. Perhaps six or seven hundred."

"The losses of the *oh-mu* are much greater!" Ilateli exclaimed excitedly, brandishing a stone spear in his hand. Ilateli had suffered a Mongauli sword-cut across his left shoulder. He wore many poultices and a disgruntled expression, but he had lost none of his fighting spirit.

"Were you hurt, chieftain?"

"It is but shallow! We of the Guro think nothing of wounds this size."

Guin turned back to Loto. "So—at least half of our force is unwounded?" he asked.

"Perhaps more than that," the Raku leader replied.

"Not bad. If we had had more casualties, then the next stage would have been difficult." Guin drank deeply from the bamboo tube that Siba handed him, and with wads of soft moss he wiped the blood and grime off his sword and body. Then he went quickly to inspect the Sem army gathered among the rocks. There were many wounded, and he did not consider their wounds light, especially considering the disadvantages they still had to overcome. Indeed, despite Ilateli's strong words, there were many Sem now lying on the rocks being tended by their friends. Yet the wildlings' morale at least had not been damaged. They believed in Guin, and in their conviction did not doubt that he was sent by the gods to save them from the Mongauli who sought to trample them into oblivion. Surely Guin would bring them victory. They remembered the words that he had spoken—"We are few, but we have a strong ally, Nospherus"—and those words still gave them strength. None questioned the power and purpose of this barren land. It was their home, and was indeed their ally.

"Riyaad, what are we to do now?" Siba asked. The Raku youth had assumed the role of leader of Guin's personal guard.

"We will do as planned," the leopard-man responded

curtly. "It will not be long before our Mongauli pursuers enter the Devil's Anvil."

"Ah, Riyaad!" one of the Sem warriors watching from atop a high rock shouted down.

"Are they here?"

"Yes!"

"Good. Tubai!"

"Yes, Riyaad!"

The Tubai women showed a sudden rush of activity. "It is our turn now! Yii yiii yyii!"

Yelling excitedly in their shrill voices, they brought out a number of glazed earthenware jugs that they had prepared. Each Tubai dame carried one to the edge of the sea of yidoh, and the jugs were spaced evenly along that edge.

The pots were full of the pure juice of the alika fruit. It had been the role of the yidoh-kin women to strain the fruits and fill these pots the night before. The Tubai did not raise the yidoh for food, nor did they keep them for any other purpose of husbandry. Their village lay in a place so infested with the creatures that they had learned these skills mainly as a way of controlling the damage that the yidoh did to them. Now their skills would be put to a new use.

"Yii yiii yii!"

Screaming as one, they tossed the contents of the pots

toward the yidoh. At once the overpowering smell of the alika juice spread out in a cloud that made even the Tubai Sem blanch and cough and rub their eyes. The effect on the yidoh was incredible. With the strength of a stormy sea they rose in trembling waves, seeking desperately to escape from the horrible stench that assailed them. Gathering speed, the monstrous tide rushed toward the southern edge of the Devil's Anvil. This was exactly as they had planned. Even so, the Sem watched in trepidation, collectively holding their breath.

"Alphetto," Loto muttered in an amazed half-whisper.

Guin, however, did not seem moved by the scene at all. He raised and lowered his hand to signal the next phase of his plan.

Now the Tubai women pulled their carven alika wood hats down in front of their faces and fastened them behind their heads with strings. Small holes to see through had been cut in the tops of the hats, which thus served as crude wooden masks. They looked very strange, these tiny bark-garbed people with featureless, round faces, but they did not remain still for their remarkable appearance to be admired. Swiftly they snatched up new jars and ran in the wake of the yidoh, chasing the rustling bulbous forms and throwing more juice at them to drive them farther along.

The rushing mass of yidoh, having gathered momentum in its fear, was moving incredibly fast, and now the sickening creatures crawled over and under each other with a chaotic, boiling

motion as each raced to escape the foul alika. So precipitous
was their movement and so indistinct their forms that even the
Tubai could not have said where one yidoh began and the next
one ended. What mattered, anyhow, was that they were all
joined in frantic, headlong flight.

With apparent calm and indifference, Guin watched the
eerie, spasmodic sea receding. When he judged that the time
was right, however, he turned with great rapidity to the Sem
behind him and spoke out sharply.

"Siba!"

"Yes, Riyaad!"

"The next stage!"

Immediately Siba and several other Sem took off at a run.
Guin watched them flash across the desert, making sure of their
timing.

"Haa!" came a happy shout from the Tubai women around
him. "The Tubai have used up two years' worth of alika!"

Astrias and Leegan, at the heads of the two columns of red
knights who now formed the vanguard of the Mongauli army,
led the pursuit of the rapidly retreating Sem. They rode hard;
and yet, even though they were on horseback and their enemies
were on foot, they couldn't close the distance between themselves and the wildlings. Their horses' hooves sank deep into

the hot sand, and oftentimes their steeds wallowed almost belly-deep in the loose dust. The fact that they carried fully armored knights did not help.

"Hyaa! Hyaa!"

The knights yanked on the reins incessantly, urging the animals forward with spur and whip.

Compared to the horses' iron-shod hooves, the flat, lightly furred feet of the Sem were perfectly adapted for running across the desert sand. Moreover, the wildlings knew the lay of the land and its many obstacles and pathways. In order to confuse their pursuers, they ran in measured zigzags but took care not to lose the Mongauli entirely in the vast sea of sand. None among the Mongauli force was aware that they were carefully being led toward some place—none save Count Marus, the keep-lord of Tauride, the commander of the two thousand blue knights who were bringing up the rear behind the foot soldiers. His thoughtful face had borne a look of deep concern ever since the Mongauli had begun their long pursuing charge.

Lieutenant Garanth, Marus's right hand and a veteran of similar age and experience, now approached to ride alongside his commander. "Lord Captain! You have a look of worry, sir. What are you thinking?"

"Those Sem run too fast," Marus replied, rocking slightly in the saddle as his horse adjusted to a change of terrain. "Or maybe it's that they're going too slow. They're moving too slow to completely evade us, and yet they're running faster than they would if they really wanted to stop and fight again before they are exhausted. It doesn't make sense. There is much that does not make sense about the Sem actions we've encountered on this expedition."

"Perhaps you are reading too much into it, my lord."

"I hope that is the case, Garanth. But if this feeling of impending danger turns out to be caused by more than just my old nerves, we may not be able to simply shrug it off—not if we find ourselves in the midst of some trap or ambush. Ever since you and I were boys of fifteen, I have been in countless battles, from skirmishes to giant wars that determined the fate of nations; if there is one thing I have learned from all that experience, Garanth, it is that battles are alive. Battles are living things. As with beasts, you must try to know them, you must handle them with care and some love, but you must never take your eyes off them, or they will go for your throat. Battles are wild beasts that can never truly be tamed, Garanth. You need both a whip and meat if you want them to turn on your foes and not yourself. The general...does not understand this."

Garanth was silent.

"The general is young, and, more importantly, she has never tasted defeat. She is a beast trainer who has never been bitten." Saying that much, Marus closed his mouth and rode for a while in silence.

A while later, however, the count looked intently at the white cloud on the horizon and muttered out loud, "I do not understand it."

"What, my lord?"

"If I knew, I would not be so troubled. This time, I fear, the creature known as 'battle' is rather unhappy with us. Wait!"

"What is it, my lord?"

"Look! What is that?" A frown creased Count Marus's craggy brow as he pointed toward the horizon.

"Is that not the white cloud of dust which shows us where the Sem are?"

"You cannot tell, Garanth? The way the dust cloud is rising—it is different from the way it moved before." The count bit his lip and thought for a moment, then suddenly pounded his saddle in exasperation. "Ah! I see now!"

"What is it, my lord?"

"We had forgotten! This is Nospherus—and Leegan and Astrias are in danger!"

"What?"

"Garanth, go! Ride ahead to Astrias and Leegan and give them the order to stop! You can inform the general later. We must halt as quickly as possible. Go!"

"Yes, sir!" Garanth galloped off promptly, still uncertain as to exactly what was going on.

"Halt! All troops, halt!" many of the blue knights now rode ahead bellowing their revered captain's order.

"What is this?" Amnelis demanded, surprised. "Those are Marus's knights, are they not?"

"Yes, General."

"What are they doing, giving orders to halt? I am the general here! Has Marus gone mad? Orders! Orders! Get Marus here at once. Quickly!"

Feldrik himself hurriedly galloped toward the rear guard.

Meanwhile, Garanth was moving forward along the advance lines of red knights as fast as he could go. "Lord Astrias! Lord Leegan, stop! Halt, now! Wait!"

Pollak heard the hoarse voice of the old knight.

"Captain!"

"I think I heard it too," Astrias said. "Someone is—"

"Garanth, Count Marus's lieutenant."

"What is he saying? Stop? Is that an order from the general?" Astrias furrowed his brow unhappily. "Very well. All troops, halt!" he shouted.

The knights of Astrias Corps demonstrated the quality of their daily training by slowing to a standstill without waiting for a second command.

Leegan Corps, however, kept up its headlong pursuit. Garanth had been racing along the right side of the vanguard of red knights. His shouts had been heard by Astrias and his men on the right, but pounding hooves and clanging armor had prevented the order from being heeded by the left wing.

"Leegan! Leegan, stop!" Seeing his friend galloping on unchecked, Astrias shouted with all his might.

It was just then that someone shouted in horror, "What in the world is that?" The fear in the voice was so palpable that the cry was impossible to ignore.

It made Astrias start. He followed the shouting knight's gaze—and froze in terror.

—— 4 ——

"Arghh!"

Down the line, terrifying screams erupted from the Mongauli knights.

"What in the name—"

"A swarm! A swarm of yidoh!"

"Pollak!" Astrias shouted to his right-hand man. "Let's get out of here! Pull back!"

The captain had done his share of time with the Marches patrol, and he knew all too well the terror of the yidoh—bizarre creatures that could not be harmed by bow or blade. "Ride!" Astrias shouted as he yanked his horse around, heading back the way he had come without thought of pride or reputation. Against a human foe, he might well have acted differently, but where the foul creatures of Nospherus were concerned, there was no such thing as pride. There was only death, and the will to evade it. Where was the honor in getting crushed by a pale lump of animated jelly?

None of the invaders, not even the most experienced Marches veterans among them, had ever seen a yidoh colony like this. As far ahead as they could gaze, the Nospherus desert was covered by a solid sheet of the deadly white ooze, frothing and bubbling, a sea of terrible hunger—and how fast it moved! It rushed like a tidal wave pushed by some tremor in the bowels of the earth. It was as if the earth itself had turned on its children in a sudden blind rage, sending a living white poison to cleanse its surface of them. Faced with the terror of the yidoh, the entire corps of trained Mongauli elites went mad with fear. In an instant knights and soldiers were transformed into a common mob, desperately fleeing for safety.

"Yidoh! Yidoh!"

"They're coming for us!"

The men farther back in the ranks saw the front lines wheeling and racing toward them. When they could make out their screams at last, they, too, turned their horses with frantic speed and galloped for the open desert beyond, occasionally stealing glances back at the rapidly approaching wave of death.

"Aaah! They're following us!" The cries cut through the rising dust behind Astrias, who was retreating now at a full gallop, his mind seized with fear. Hearing another horrible scream, he chanced a look over his shoulder just in time to see something which made the bile rise in his throat and the tears come to his eyes.

"Help! Hel—"

Behind him, Leegan's red knights were being swallowed by the wave of yidoh. They had not heard Garanth's warning, and by the time they had noticed that something was amiss in the desert before them, it was too late. The pale, fluid creatures were already coming for them at full speed, and they had no time to turn around.

The yidoh overran Leegan Corps like an avalanche overwhelming careless mountaineers. First the horses' legs were caught in the shivering violent jelly, and the beasts stumbled and fell with baffled whinnies of terror. As the steeds went down, the red knights who rode them were thrown, and faster than they could stand, the undulating, writhing, ravenous death engulfed horse and rider. The muffled screams and cries of the men being crushed sounded like the calls of perverse spirits through the muffling blanket of jelly. At the edges of the advancing yidoh, those who had tried to flee to either side were inexorably caught and dragged down, swallowed by the living mucous that crawled across their faces even as they reached in desperation for their companions' extended hands. Soon all troops within the yidoh's reach had been dragged under; knight after knight, shrieking and struggling, was sucked into that white hell.

Astrias saw what was happening to Leegan's knights and quaked with fear. Suddenly he found his voice and shouted in dismay: "Leegan! Leegan is down!" He could see his friend's horse, a handsome bay, kicking the air as the yidoh flowed around it. On the rearing steed was Leegan, his figure frozen in fear and desperation.

"Rescue!" screamed Astrias, and foolishly he turned his horse and attempted to gallop back toward the hive alone. But Pollak, who had been riding close behind him, cut him off with his horse.

"Out of my way, Leegan is in danger!"

"No—it is too dangerous!"

Astrias reached for Pollak's reins to try and jerk the other's horse aside, but Pollak grabbed his hand and pushed it back.

"No, sir. It is too dangerous."

Astrias's bloodshot eyes met Pollak's. Both men were as pale as corpses, and each was tense with fear and the fierce weight of his duty.

"No," Pollak pleaded, his voice cracking. "I beg you, sir, no."

"But, Leegan! It's Leegan!"

"It is too dangerous! We must escape!"

Pollak let go of his captain's hand and, without asking permission, slapped the flank of Astrias's horse with the flat of his sword. Wheeling toward safety, the horse bolted away at top speed. Astrias, now clinging to his crazed steed's neck, shouted "Leegan!" once more, then began to scream out curses against the Nospheran wilds. His shouts, the cries of other knights calling for fallen friends, and the whinnies of the dying horses drowned out the sound of bones being crushed by the yidoh.

The swarm of yidoh had begun to change color. No longer pale white, they now showed through their translucent bodies the armor of the red and black knights they had swallowed. More dimly visible within their writhing bodies were the fragmentary forms of their victims, already so crushed that their original shapes were no longer discernible; the hive was blotched scarlet from the blood they had sucked from human and horse. Here and there among the yidoh was one so swollen from the prey it had swallowed that it bulged huge and taut as a vast and hellish pustule. To these amorphous creatures, against whom cold steel blades were harmless and armor offered scant defense, the pride of Mongaul were merely an exquisite and plentiful prey.

So horrible was the sight of the feeding monsters that, even when the surviving soldiers realized that the things seemed to have ceased their pursuit, they did not stop running. The entire invading army had lost its self-control to fear.

"Halt! Halt! Black Knights, halt!"

"What is this? Four great knightly orders, the very pride of

Mongaul, running in fear from the no-man's-land's primitive monstrosities?"

Finally the surviving captains calmed their own nerves and, cursing under their breath, sought to control their troops.

"This is a shame we will bear for many generations!"

"Calm down! You—stop your horses! Get back into formation!"

"Halt! Can you not hear me?"

Furiously the commanders galloped back and forth, waving their whips in an attempt to cut off the frenzied knights and their stampeding horses. For it was not just the soldiers but their steeds as well that were reluctant to arrest their flight. Indeed, many of the knights were now grasping fiercely at the reins, trying to regain control of their mounts, while other fellow cavalrymen had been thrown or were being dragged by the stirrups.

"Stop! Why don't you stop?!"

Still roiling upon the desert sands, the hive of yidoh had slowed and spread out across the scene of the debacle. Distant as they now were, the surviving Mongauli could still hear the gruesome sounds of their comrades being devoured.

"What is going on?"

Despairing of ever regaining order, the lords and captains sought for the lady-general that she might give them directions. Had the Dragon Knights of Cheironia assailed them, or the deadly Tiger Knights, or the faithful of Niroc who fought with hurricane-blades, the Mongauli troops would not have been afraid. But here in the wildlands of Nospherus, they had discovered that they had neither a place to hide nor any means of fighting the horrendously alien creature. That knowledge unmanned them.

"We must find the lady Amnelis!"

"The general will give us the right order—she'll know how to handle the situation."

"What shall we do?"

The soldiers, finding that their training and experience had failed them, now looked for their general like children looking for their loving mother.

But Amnelis, sitting on her horse atop a rise in the land apart from the main body of her army, had gone whiter than the armor and cloak she wore.

"Oh, how horrible this is!"

General though she was, she was still a girl of eighteen. She had maintained her legendary self-control, but it required her utmost effort to hide her trembling and unease from those around her.

"How fearsome are these 'yidoh'! Marus, Marus!"

"Yes?"

"What are they? I have never seen nor even imagined anything so horrible. Is this some fiendish devilry brought on by the Sem, or do horrid creatures like that just wander the sands of Nospherus?"

"Alas, such things are denizens here," Count Marus replied. He had left his corps in order to protect the lady-general. "I only wish that I had realized the danger sooner. I beg your forgiveness."

"But tell me: what are those things? Is there no way of driving them away? I am unfamiliar with creatures of this sort. But you, Marus, have been long on the Marches patrol, and you know of these things—do you not? If these monsters will not die by bowshot or blade—"

"I am afraid that is so."

"Then they are a barrier to us—we will have to go around them!"

"Yes."

Amnelis had gathered her officers around her for an emergency council of war. In addition to Count Marus, Gajus Runecaster was there, and Cal Moru, and the three captains of the white knights—Vlon, Lindrot, and Feldrik—whose faces were pale and haggard. Amnelis looked to each of them, hoping for answers to her questions, but each man as she looked at him hung his head in shame at his own powerlessness.

Just then Astrias, who had finished rounding up his forces, galloped up with Pollak at his side to give their report.

"General!" Seeing the young lady-general surrounded by her knights, Astrias breathed a sigh of relief. "You are well!"

"Losses?" Amnelis quickly regained her icy manner of supreme authority, and her voice was harsh.

Astrias replied without strength. "Leegan Corps took extremely heavy losses. My losses, too, are heavy, though not as bad as his. Viscount Leegan himself..."

"Leegan?" asked Amnelis.

Astrias's long face shook with sorrow, and he choked on his words as he spoke. "The yidoh, they..."

Count Marus raised his voice in pain. "So the viscount is dead."

"Fire!" sputtered Cal Moru suddenly.

"What?" Amnelis looked over her shoulder.

Suddenly everyone turned to look at the mysterious spell-caster who had crossed the desert alone. Cal Moru's hideous face remained hidden in his hood, but he raised his skeletal arm and pointed towards the yidoh. "The yidoh's weakness is fire, my general. That is the only thing that can kill them. You cannot pierce a yidoh with a blade, but with fire..."

"Yes, of course!"

Depressed though the commanders were by the loss of

Leegan, son of Ricard, the life returned to their faces at this hint of a means to fight back against their bizarre foe.

"Yes, fire!"

"Good thinking, Cal Moru!" Amnelis had calmed down as well. Out here in the wildlands, surrounded by the many unknown terrors of Nospherus, she had for a short time lost her confidence and had let herself become too much like any other fearful, worrying girl who had not quite attained womanhood. But now the shine of the proud and haughty Lady of Mongaul returned to her eyes. Whether her recovery owed more to the fact that Cal Moru had remembered the yidoh's weakness, or whether it was because the young and handsome Astrias was now standing next to her, clearly as worshipping as ever, she herself did not know.

"Feldrik!"

"Yes, my lady!"

"Orders!"

"Yes, my lady!"

"The yidoh are vulnerable to fire! You will command the men to take all the torches from their packs and gather all the wood they can find, and prepare to drive off the yidoh colony with fire."

"As you wish, my lady!"

"Marus!"

"Yes, my lady!"

"Return to your blue knights and gather them up. Astrias!"

Astrias looked surprised. "My lady!"

Amnelis's mysterious emerald gaze met the glint of Astrias's deep black eyes. She gave him a cold look; but then, seeing that this had set him on the verge of tears, she faltered. When at last she spoke, however, it was with an authority that made Lindrot and Vlon, standing nearby, wither at the force of it.

"Astrias, you disappoint me. You disobeyed my orders during the battle today. This is your second failure in nearly as many days. Are you really the one they call the 'Red Lion of Alvon'?" Astrias jerked as though he had been struck by a whip. But Amnelis, heedless, continued, "Fail me a third time, and you can consider your captain's badge gone. Understood?"

"Yes...my lady."

"Now, go—gather up the remnants of Leegan Corps, add them to yours, and fall back to the rear."

"...I beg you not to assign me to rearguard duty, my lady."

Amnelis's eyes flared up. "Will you have me repeat myself?"

"N-No."

Vlon and Lindrot looked with compassion at the drooping Astrias as he headed back reluctantly to his troops.

The Mongauli army, beginning to recover from its shock, began to swing back into action.

"A battle to avenge the fallen!"

"Death to the yidoh that killed our friends!"

"Fire! We'll put fire to the filthy things!"

The footmen dropped their spears, the knights dismounted, and the bowmen laid aside their bows. Together all the warriors of Mongaul gathered everything burnable that they could find in the barren wastes. They prepared oil in pots, and they made a giant bonfire from which they spread the flame to their torches.

Meanwhile, the sun was beginning to dip into the west. A thin purple mist had begun to flow around the invaders' army, tinting the crooked lines of the wasteland around them with sickly hues of death. Only half a tad away, the Mongauli could see the colony of yidoh, quiescent now and looking as if it had finished digesting all its prey, no longer moving but lying low and flat as a calm sea. The men could feel the presence of those amorphous creatures like a slumbering nightmare waiting for its chance to rage again.

"If we cannot drive off the yidoh before nightfall, we're in trouble," one soldier observed, spitting on the sand. His unease was shared by all those around him. And as though to justify that unease, a cry rang out...

"The Sem!!"

In no time, every Mongauli was shouting.

"They've returned!"

"Aaah! They're here!"

Count Marus bit his lip and slapped his knee with his sword. "I knew it! The sly monkeys!"

Sem with eerie face-paintings came streaming down the sand dunes that were already fading in the dusk—two bands, a nightmarish vision, one from the left and one from the right.

"Aiii aii aii!"

"Hyaaa ai!"

"Yii yii yii!"

"They were waiting for the yidoh to distract us!" Count Marus shouted. "Men! To arms! Don't let the monkeys beat us again!"

"Mongaul! Mongaul!" shouted his men.

But just then yet another cry rang out. "Aaah! The yidoh move again!" This terrified shout was followed by a sound like rolling thunder. It was the sound of the yidoh rumbling along the ground, approaching fast.

The Tubai, creeping up to the far side of the vast yidoh colony, had poured the alika juice a third time, prompting the entire mass of yidoh to move. The amorphous creatures were at the end of their tethers, crazed by the smell of blood and the hated alika smell.

Yidoh from the front. From the left and right, ape-men.

"Ah...you crafty...grr..." the old warrior Marus grit his teeth and snarled helplessly. He lowered his faceplate with a snap, fixed his neckplate to ward off the rain of Sem poison arrows that was already beginning, and drew his sword with a wild flourish. Then the veteran of countless battles charged toward the enemies now approaching from the left.

"Keep-lord!"

"The count is in danger!"

The blue knights wheeled around on their horses and followed after their leader. In a flash, hand-to-hand battle was joined for the third time that day.

"The yidoh! Help, the yidoh!"

"Fire! Use fire!"

Both Irrim and Tangard Corps had fallen into mass confusion. Holding torches in their hands, they had been about to head for the yidoh when they realized that the approaching jelly-things were too many and coming too fast for them to combat effectively. Then, even as they raised their torches to fight the yidoh as best they could, a hail of Sem arrows came down on them. Men holding torches aloft in the growing gloom made perfect targets for the wildlings. Many a soldier was stricken by an arrow during the first few moments of battle and fell into the onrushing wave of the yidoh.

"Fire! Use fire!"

"Marus! Marus!" Amnelis shouted.

"Lady General, this place is too dangerous. The yidoh are close!"

Gajus and the captains of the general's guard, Vlon and Lindrot, insisted that she move, and quickly she pulled back, protected by her flag-bearers.

"You...you...you!" she grit her teeth and spat. "Using the yidoh! How cowardly! Using the beasts! You...Guin!"

Just then, Gajus touched her arm to get her attention.

Amnelis looked up, and was stricken with unwilling awe.

The evening sun had become a giant orange disk balanced on the blade of the horizon, and against that backdrop, as though he were the Sun God Ruah himself, a warrior had appeared striding over the dune's sandy crest. Behind him were arrayed the elite of the Sem. Guin's leopard head formed a dark silhouette edged in flame as he gazed down on the battle beginning to play out below him.

"Guin..." Amnelis's voice became a fiery breath across her lips. Her mesmerizing green eyes shone. Without blinking she gazed at that heroic silhouette, as perfect as though a master's hand had chiselled it out of eternal stone.

Guin lifted his hand—and brought it down without a word.

"Riyaad! Riyaad!" rose howling cries from the Sem, "RIYAAD!" The leopard-headed avatar of war and his five hundred brave wildling warriors charged forward like a storm to the sound of that earth-shattering war cry. Irresistibly they came on, heading straight for the melee between the Sem forces and Marus's blue-armored troops, driving into the heart of the fray like a bolt of lighting.

Within moments, Guin's mighty sword was swinging in wide arcs to left and to right, reaping the bloody harvest of war.

"Vlon, save Marus!" Amnelis yelled. "Nay...I shall go in myself!" Then, at the head of her personal guard of one thousand knights clad in white, not one of whom had been lost, she galloped headlong into battle.

The battle had risen to a terrible intensity far beyond that of the previous clashes—a high tide of destruction in which the Mongauli army, the Sem combined forces, and the undulating yidoh fought with the violence of the damned. The flames in the hands of the Mongauli burned bright red. Screams, battle cries, shrieks of pain and death, the ringing of swords and the flowing of blood all mingled in one fearsome crescendo of war that seemed to have no end, a roaring flood that flowed out across the vast Nospherus wasteland.

Above it all, the giant sun dipped slowly, as though it meant to envelop them all. Deeper and deeper burned its crimson, ready to paint the entire world the color of blood.

END OF BOOK THREE